"Love has to ... chin lifted ... mean having ... yo..."

"Love also involves responsibility, and that's something you obviously couldn't handle. Maybe you still can't ... maybe that's why you prance around with a phony name, making up stories about where yôu come from. Maybe you're just as selfish and immature as you were the day you ran away from me."

"And you're just as thick-headed on the subject," Laurel shot back, cursing the heat that flooded her cheeks in response to Sawyer's angry taunts.

"No. I'm even worse. I've had a good long time to stew about it. Only now I don't take no for an answer as easily as I did then."

"You never took it easily," she murmured, but it was as if he didn't hear. His gaze held hers prisoner as he lifted his hands to her face, cradling her delicate chin and flushed cheeks with his strong, narrow fingers.

"You see, I've also had a lot of time to learn how to get what I want ... everything I want," he added, leaning even closer. "You'd do well to remember that, *Laurel*. I've had to work and scrape and fight for everything I've ever wanted, but in the end, I always get it."

Then his mouth came down hard to claim hers ...

Liz Grady

Born in Providence, Rhode Island, Liz Grady has lived in that state ever since. In college she majored in English and education—and met her husband, whom she married three days after graduation. For the next three and a half years she taught school—in her words, "more than long enough to know I was in the wrong profession."

With two young sons at home, Liz soon decided she needed to do more than cook, clean, and fingerpaint. An avid romance reader, she tried her hand at writing. She claims she owes her sense of humor to her maternal grandmother ("a very wise and witty woman" who lived with her family while Liz was growing up), and she credits much of her success in her new career to her very supportive husband and adaptable children.

The author of nine books so far, lately Liz finds little time for her hobbies—quilting, cross-stitch embroidery, and reading—but she says her writing makes the sacrifice worthwhile. "Every day I marvel at my good fortune in being able to work at something I enjoy so much!"

Dear Reader:

We're very excited to be able to offer you author Mary Modean's first book for Second Chance at Love, the deeply moving *In Name Only* (#400). Threatened with losing custody of her son Mike, Leslie Burgess flees the east coast, seeking refuge in rural Oklahoma and a marriage of convenience to rancher and veterinarian David Nichols. Sublimating past sorrows, David and Leslie work hard to pull their lives together. But he's trapped by a secret burden of pain he's afraid to share...and she's unprepared for the soul-stirring depth of desire this lean, quiet man arouses within her. Mary Modean delivers with emotionally complex characters whose compelling—and very real—love story will leave you anxious for more from this talented author.

You won't be disappointed in Liz Grady's fresh take on a "coming to terms with the past" theme in this month's *Reclaim the Dream* (#401). Washington protocol expert Laurel Forrest seems the perfect product of a classy upbringing, moving through the corridors of power with ease and sophistication...until her long-ago love, brawny maverick Sawyer Gates shows up and threatens to shatter her facade. Only Sawyer knows the lie she's built her life on, and Laurel's got to finagle her way out of being exposed. But somehow the heat of Sawyer's gaze sparks a need, and Laurel's not sure she wants to escape the danger of his strong embrace...Liz Grady leads you through a maze of love and deception to a delightfully satisfying conclusion in this, her ninth, Second Chance at Love.

Carolina Moon (#402) by Joan Darling combines exciting romance with hilarious domestic comedy for surefire entertainment. When the man of her dreams moves next door and proceeds to sweep her off her feet, Eileen "Fergie" Duffy can scarcely believe her good fortune. But her ardent neighbor, Ryan O'Donnell, has no use for children—and Fergie, a widow, happens to be the mother of three! Her kids adore Ryan, though; they unanimously decide to adopt him—and every time Ryan looks at Fergie, his resolve crumbles. The house next door starts to feel like home, and Fergie's the one woman who can make him happy...Author Joan Darling confesses she based Ryan on *Moonlighting's* Bruce Willis, and he's certainly a hunk with a sense of humor, not to mention fatal charm.

Diana Morgan exhibits more marvelous madness this month with *The Wedding Belle* (#403). Intrigued by a mysterious blonde decked out in bridal finery while she is stationed in the middle of the Chattahoochee River, patrician venture capitalist Ned Fontaine introduces himself. Soon he's introducing Jolie MacGregor to his family as *his* bride in a nonmarriage of convenience. Ned will stake Jolie as she opens a high-fashion boutique, while she'll keep unmarried Southern belles and their anxious mamas away from Ned. This perfect arrangement takes some interesting turns when Ned and Jolie fall madly in love! With the heady mist of a fine champagne, Diana Morgan presents a characteristically memorable romantic romp.

Laine Allen brings lively romance to a department store setting in *Courting Trouble* (#404), when Personnel Manager Claire Kendrick takes on an ex-convict as an employee. Mace Dawson's good looks are truly criminal—and his answers to the company questionnaire are downright impertinent. Claire's boss insists it will do this con-man good to work under her protective wing—but it's Claire's heart that needs protection when Mace starts to undo all her rules and regulations. Claire doesn't know that Mace is merely masquerading as a man in need of reform; he's actually the head of an outreach program for ex-convicts, and wants to learn how it feels to be a second-class citizen. Claire's already falling fast— and there's plenty of first-class banter as these two *try* to work together...

A widowed mother finds love again in *Everybody's Hero* (#405) by Second Chance star Jan Mathews. Delaney Anderson never wanted her seventeen-year-old son to join the Marines—and she certainly never expected to fall in love with his recruiting officer! Captain Lloyd Thomas is an officer and a gentleman, but Delaney's past with the military is a tragic one. She's afraid her years of heartbreak won't let her give in to Lloyd's sense of fun, yet he soon lures her into a schoolgirl's romance that leaves her breathless. Delaney learns to give up some of her maternal obligations, and Jan portrays her passionate rejuvenation with grace and good-natured humor. *Everybody's Hero* is another winner from an all-time Second Chance favorite, topping off a month of spring surprises.

Happy Reading!

Joan Marlow

Joan Marlow, Editor
SECOND CHANCE AT LOVE
The Berkley Publishing Group
200 Madison Avenue
New York, NY 10016

SECOND CHANCE AT LOVE™

LIZ GRADY
RECLAIM THE DREAM

A
SECOND CHANCE AT LOVE
BOOK

**For Beth Madden and Kristen O'Connor.
And for Sue Munroe, with appreciation for all the kind
words and encouragement.**

Second Chance at Love books are published by
The Berkley Publishing Group
200 Madison Avenue, New York, NY 10016

Chapter One

No DOUBT ABOUT it, Laurel Forrest was on a roll. From the bleak beginnings that she rarely thought about these days, she had worked and plotted and angled herself into quite a prestigious position as special assistant in the State Department's Office of Protocol. Quietly elegant cocktail parties, such as the one going on around her, where talk of agendas and interfaces flowed as freely as the champagne and Perrier, were all part of her fast-paced routine in the lofty, insider's world of Washington, D.C.

And in a few weeks—two months, tops—and definitely before her thirtieth birthday, still a half a year away, she would be resigning her coveted position for one even more noteworthy: wife of the United States ambassador to Great Britain. True, Jasper hadn't formally announced their engagement yet. Hadn't, if you wanted to get technical, even formally proposed yet. But he would—as soon as the Senate Foreign Relations

Committee had confirmed his appointment. Of that, Laurel was certain. Her marriage to Jasper would be the final domino in a long, neatly fallen row.

Wife of the ambassador to the Court of St. James's. Quite a feat for a woman who ten years earlier had fled poverty and a dismal future in Beaumont, Texas, and arrived in London with the grand sum of $62.71 tucked away in her sky-blue vinyl billfold. That trip had been the modest start to the uphill roll that had propelled Laurel—or rather permitted her to propel herself—to where she was today, poised on the brink of success. So why couldn't she shake this feeling of impending doom? It was almost as if the hand of fate were hovering above her life, waiting to pluck victory from her grasp at the last second.

Only, Laurel didn't believe in such notions as fate or undying love or happily ever after. She believed in working hard and making her own opportunities, and so far that creed had served her well. Soon she would be Mrs. Jasper Dane, and all her dreams of security and position and wealth would be fulfilled.

Nodding as if fascinated by whatever the two high-achiever types she was standing with were discussing, Laurel let her eyes skim the surrounding sea of red "power ties" and Britches-of-Georgetown tweed until she located Jasper across the room. At fifty-five he was still a fit and energetic-looking man. Although neither very tall nor unusually handsome—his curly silver hair and year-round tan were his most striking physical attributes—he still managed to turn heads whenever he entered a room by projecting an air of absolute power. Probably because he'd wielded it so well for so long. As the publisher of newspapers in several key cities throughout the country, Jasper Dane was a very wealthy, very influential man, and a perfect choice to be named to the most prestigious U.S. ambassadorship.

And thanks to her earlier experience working at the

American embassy in London, Laurel was the perfect choice to be his wife.

Excusing herself with the air of polite regret she'd perfected over the years, Laurel started across the marble-floored room to join Jasper. Her stride took on a subtle, determined briskness as she drew closer and identified the small group of Washington power brokers gathered around him. Usually she treated such men with polite caution, recognizing them for the necessary nuisance they were. This particular party, however, was being given in Jasper's honor by Marjorie Wilshire, the grand dame of Washington society, so that he could meet and charm key members of Congress prior to the confirmation hearings—not so that he could spend the evening cornered by those constantly seeking to curry his favor.

Fortunately, the sort of smooth maneuver required to shake them was Laurel's specialty. Years of pampering diplomats and handling arrangements for state visits had rendered her a master of the art of stepping on toes and twisting arms without hurting feelings . . . a talent not likely to be overlooked by either Jasper or those considering his worthiness to serve as ambassador. Off the record, Laurel just might be the factor to tip the scales in his favor.

She moved in the inner social circles of Washington as if she'd been born to it. Perhaps even better, because she had to try harder . . . staying constantly on her toes, watching her rear flank, making sure everything from the clothes she wore to the car she drove was exactly right.

Like tonight, for instance. Her black dress was alluring enough to draw a man's eye without alienating the conservative society matrons who had the power to make Laurel's life a bed of roses—or one of nails. Strikingly plain except for the sheer lace sleeves and neckline, the dress's narrow line complemented her willowy body. Her long, light brown hair was gathered into a loose chignon, focusing attention on her eyes. Wide-set and shimmering pale green in color, her eyes were the only feature Laurel considered remarkable in what she regarded as an otherwise ordinary face and average figure. The fact that others disagreed with her own dour assessment of her attributes seemed to her only proof that she was a whiz at creating illusions.

Illusion or not, however, Laurel was satisfied with her appearance. She knew the overall effect—one of feminine sophistication with a strong current of intelligence—was an important thread in the magic carpet that would ultimately take her where she wanted to go. Coming to a stop beside Jasper, she touched his arm with exactly the right degree of familiarity.

"Laurel." There was pride and approval in the smile Jasper directed at her. "I was just about to come looking for you."

"Then I'm glad I saved you the trouble. I thought if I could steal you away from these gentlemen for a while, we might sample some of Marjorie's hors d'oeuvres." Inclining her head toward a long table laden with an array of hot and cold food, she added, "Rumor has it she included shrimp just for you."

"Then I guess I'd better show my appreciation by eating my share. If you gentlemen will excuse us?"

The other three men nodded and murmured proper, polite responses as she and Jasper made their escape. Laurel chuckled inwardly at the phoniness of the whole thing and wondered if the rest of them were mentally chuckling and rolling their eyes, too, even as they delivered their lines. It wasn't the sort of thing she could discuss with Jasper.

They had almost reached the buffet table when Marjorie Wilshire descended upon them. A fast-moving cloud of orchid chiffon and perfectly coiffured silver hair, Marjorie had eyes that gleamed like those of a woman with a mission. And her mission at the moment was to see that her friend the President wasn't publicly embarrassed by having his choice for ambassador rejected by the Senate committee.

"Jasper, there you are. There's someone over here I think you should meet." She linked her arm through Jasper's, then turned to bring Laurel into smile range. "You, too, Laurel. He's a friend of Mike Riordon's."

Her meaning was clear. Texas Senator Mike Riordon was one of those quietly opposed to Jasper's appointment.

"Is this friend also a constituent of his?" inquired Jasper.

Marjorie nodded, her carefree smile still in place. "He's rather young but, from what I hear, capable of throwing a lot of weight in the wrong direction. It seems he's made a great deal of money very quickly in offshore drilling explorations."

"And he wants to make sure the next ambassador to Great Britain will facilitate drilling in the North Sea?"

"Exactly," countered the older woman in response to Jasper's weary-sounding question. "Now, Jasper, even if you don't favor such a position, you could practice being diplomatic by..."

Laurel's attention wandered as the other two lapsed into yet another quiet, hurried discussion of strategy. It wasn't necessary that she know every detail about every potential crisis in order to help Jasper win over the reluctant members of the committee. As she scanned the room she automatically picked out others he must be sure to speak to before the evening was over, mentally noting who could be dealt a simple hello and who should be offered enthusiastic congratulations for a granddaughter's graduation from law school. Then, without warning, her gaze was snagged by the back view of a man in a dark suit on the far side of the room.

Laurel was never certain what it was about the man

that triggered the reaction. Maybe it was the way he held himself with a kind of casual confidence that said he was comfortable with his body, and with himself. Or maybe it was the thick black hair that curled just over his shirt collar, or the way he stood while listening to someone speak—head angled a little to one side, chin up, as if he were sifting each word through some private system of defenses. Whatever it was, it had the power to plummet her back in time, making her breath catch deep in her throat, and filling her mind with a searing image of Sawyer Gates.

Of course, the logical part of her brain realized that the thirty-two-year-old Sawyer might bear little resemblance to the twenty-year-old she'd known. By now he might well have a pot belly and a balding head and look nothing at all like the man across the room. But knowing that didn't change her automatic responses one bit. Like a mother who loses a child, then through the years silently notes the growth and accomplishments of other children the same age, so Laurel's heart had kept track of Sawyer.

Far from remaining frozen at the post-adolescent age she remembered, the image she carried of him had been modified over the past eleven years. From observing other men, she'd painted in the details of age, adding lines around his eyes, more hair to his chest, and not flab but solidity to his lean frame. At first she'd tried to fight the compulsion to do it, thinking it only kept the pain alive. Finally, though, she'd come to accept it. The same way she'd come to accept the fact that in some crazy, unexplainable way, Sawyer Gates was as much a part of her present as he was of her past. And probably always would be.

". . . seems obvious that Laurel can be a real help in—shall we say—persuading these young mavericks that you can be trusted. Don't you agree, Laurel, dear?"

Laurel turned back to Marjorie with a smile. "Of

course. Mavericks were considered something of a specialty of mine when I worked in London."

"You see?" She beamed at Jasper. "Now come along both of you, before the good senator thinks we're conspiring against him."

The good senator, thought Laurel, as she and Jasper trailed along in the other woman's wake, would have to be incredibly naive not to know that that's exactly what they were doing. But it hardly mattered. Without a doubt, he and his wealthy, influential young friend were busy doing the very same thing. When Marjorie drew to a halt beside Riordon, Laurel realized that the maverick she was to bring into line was none other than the man in the dark suit, and, ridiculously, she felt her pulse quicken. Then, in a rapid stream of events, Mike Riordon was shaking hands with Jasper as Marjorie rattled off introductions, and the man turned to Laurel, his perfunctory smile quickly fading into shock as their eyes met.

It was as if a cyclone had blown through the room. Laurel felt like poor Dorothy in *The Wizard of Oz*, being swept off to a distant land where she didn't want to go. The protective shield of the last eleven years was ripped away, and with it, it seemed, all of her poise and glib sophistication. She was suddenly tongue-tied, sweaty-palmed, and face to face with her past as she stared up into the stunned, dark blue eyes of Sawyer Gates.

Chapter Two

IT WASN'T AS if Laurel hadn't prepared for this moment.

She had rehearsed the scene in her mind a hundred times in case she was ever unfortunate enough to encounter someone who remembered her from the days when she still had been known as Pandora Milinkus, the youngest daughter of a weak, dispirited mother and a drunken father. She'd even gone so far as to practice the smile and expression of polite confusion she should employ. Cordially, she would shrug, murmur something about everyone having a double somewhere, and then beat a smooth, hasty retreat. But never in her imagined scenarios had that "someone" from her past been Sawyer Gates.

Now, despite her best efforts to prepare, she was blowing it, not handling the moment with anything near the composure Sawyer was managing. His shocked reaction had been so fleeting no one else in the group appeared to have even noticed, which helped slightly to quell Laurel's panic, and she felt her heart settle back into its normal position in her chest. She barely heard the rest of the introductions, aware only of Sawyer and the way he was watching her through narrowed eyes, the slight upward tilt of his lips doing little to mask his air of sardonic amusement. She understood why he was so amused when her head finally cleared enough for her to realize that Marjorie was in the midst of an embarrassingly fawning monologue of which Laurel was the subject.

"... not one to stand in anyone's shadow, our Laurel. An absolute rarity in these days when young people seem to have thrown all notion of social etiquette to the wind. Why, I don't know how I would have managed this evening's little gala without her help. As I've always said, breeding shows."

Laurel held her breath waiting for Sawyer's response to that little gem. With one word he could shake the very foundation of the life she'd built, destroying years of hard work and careful planning. And the worst of it was that he had good reason to do exactly that. What fine revenge it would be. Instead, though, he stretched his smile into something that appeared to be a few degrees warmer and extended his right hand.

"Miss ... Forrest, is it?" At Laurel's slight nod, he continued, "It's a pleasure to meet you."

Laurel felt weak with relief. "The pleasure's mutual, Mr. Gates."

"Please. Call me Sawyer."

"Sawyer."

"And may I call you ..."—his eyes flashed—"Laurel?"

He was still holding her hand in his, leaving Laurel with no graceful way of breaking the physical contact that was sending disorienting little ripples of excitement through her. She dropped her gaze to the knot of his silk paisley tie, wondering how the others could help but

notice the awkwardness between them. "Of course . . .
Laurel would be fine."

The few seconds of silence that followed were no
doubt a perfectly ordinary pause, but they felt like an
eternity to Laurel.

Sawyer. What on earth was he doing here? And why,
after all this time, did just the sight of him dry up her
reservoir of witty, conversational remarks and make her
heart slam wildly against her ribs? She doubted she
could speak normally at the moment even if she could
think of anything to say. All she could do was stand
there, smiling limply and doing her best to avoid Sawyer's probing gaze. Her relief when Marjorie finally
started to speak again was short-lived.

"Laurel is originally from Texas, too, Sawyer," the
older woman announced. "What was the name of that
little town where you grew up, dear?"

"Beaumont," Laurel had no choice but to admit.
"But it's not all that little."

Mike Riordon glanced at Sawyer. "Beaumont? That's
Sawyer's hometown, too."

"Maybe you two have some old friends in common,"
Jasper suggested. "Although Laurel doesn't seem to
have too many ties to her past."

"That's right," Laurel quickly concurred. "It's been
years since I was anywhere near Texas."

"I know," Sawyer commented. He twisted his lips
into a smile as her gaze jerked back to meet his and
added, "You have no trace of a drawl."

The slow, smooth quality of his own voice tugged at
something buried deep inside Laurel, and suddenly she
wasn't quite so proud of the unaccented speech she'd
struggled to achieve.

"Still, Beaumont's not all that big, either," continued
Sawyer. "We just might know some of the same people.
What part of town were you from, Laurel?" The empha-
sis he placed on her name was subtle, but it was there.

"Seaside," she tossed back, eyeing him defiantly as she named the most elite section of the Gulf Coast town. It was several miles and a world in lifestyle from the run-down neighborhood where she'd actually lived, sharing the single tiny bedroom with her two sisters while her parents slept on a pullout sofa in the living room.

"Ah, Seaside," Sawyer echoed. "I'm afraid that's too rich for my blood. All of my friends grew up in Darlington, just as I did." He turned his smile on Marjorie. "I see what you mean about breeding, Mrs. Wilshire."

Damn him! Laurel gritted her teeth behind a smile. It was his choice whether to expose her or go along with her charade, but he had no right to bait her that way. Lord knew the next few moments would be hard enough to get through without him intentionally setting hurdles in her way. Fortunately, the discussion of Sawyer's and her shared past seemed to have run its course, and Marjorie had progressed to grilling him, in the aggressively gracious manner only she could manage, about his reason for being in Washington. She's searching for his Achilles' heel, Laurel thought, and she wondered if he'd developed one over the years.

"So you're combining business with pleasure," Marjorie was saying to him. "Very wise. Too many men don't appreciate the virtue of relaxation. And you've chosen the perfect city for it, I might add. Granted, I'm a bit biased, but Washington has something to offer everyone. Ballet, the symphony, art galleries . . ."

Laurel watched Sawyer closely as Marjorie continued, curious to see what his response would be to the mention of all those cultural activities she'd had to teach herself to appreciate. His polite indifference was exactly what she'd expected—and, Laurel discovered, it pleased her. Sawyer really was a maverick and always had been. Wealthy and successful he might now be, but she liked knowing that underneath that fancy, hand-

tailored suit he was still the same self-confident noncon-
formist she'd once loved.

The Sawyer she'd known had been nothing like the
other men in this room, so hungry for power that they
would befriend anyone, conform to any standard, to get
it. And it appeared he hadn't changed much. Laurel was
willing to bet that when you mentioned music, Sawyer
still thought first of a steel guitar, not a string quartet,
and when you mentioned sports, he thought of no-
holds-barred, Texas-variety football, not nine holes of
golf played on a perfectly manicured course.

Inside her, a surge of affection welled up for the man
that he was, followed hard on its heels by a chilling
sadness. It was true that he hadn't changed, but she had.
She suddenly realized that, even now, standing so close
that she could touch him with only a slight movement of
her arm, they were light-years apart. And what separated them was something more unconquerable than either time or distance, something she herself had created.
As surely as she had created Laurel Forrest. Suddenly it
was hard for her to breathe in the crowded room.

She touched Jasper's arm lightly. "Excuse me for a
moment, please. I won't be long."

She looked up to find Sawyer's gaze focused on the
spot where her fingers rested on Jasper's sleeve. Almost
guiltily, without thinking, she jerked her hand away,
earning a quick, knowing look of contempt from Sawyer. It was obvious what he thought, and the injustice of
it flamed in Laurel's cheeks as she turned and made her
way out of the room. He thought that poor Pandora had
changed her name, spit-shined her image, and set her
sights on snagging a rich older man for a husband. Well,
it wasn't true.

At least, not exactly. It was true that Jasper was rich
and older than she, and it was true that she wanted the
respect and security that would be hers as his wife. But
she wasn't duping him or coddling his aging male ego

in order to get it. She was offering in return not undying love or burning passion, but something Jasper wanted and needed much more: her experience and talent at navigating the diplomatic circles he was about to enter. And although their relationship had never been discussed in exactly those calculated terms, Laurel was confident that Jasper understood the reality of their situation as well as she did.

The first-floor bathroom was occupied, so Laurel opted for the next best place to rally her defenses, the small terrace off Marjorie's sitting room. Separated from the main patio by a screen of shrubbery, it afforded the privacy she needed to plan her strategy for the rest of the evening.

Could she possibly be lucky enough to avoid Sawyer completely for the remainder of the party? Laurel doubted it. Obviously, he would be as curious about her activities over the past eleven years as she was about his. Probably even more so. After all, all he'd done was become wealthy—she'd become a whole new person. And if there was one thing she remembered about Sawyer, it was his determination. If he wanted to talk with her, all her best, most fleet-footed maneuvers wouldn't stop him.

If avoiding him completely was out, the next safest course would be to avoid having to answer his questions within earshot of anyone else. It was going to be difficult enough explaining to him why she'd done what she had without having to worry about being overheard. Laurel stared into the distant sky where lights from the Capitol created a hazy glow, and wondered exactly how much she should tell him. Could she trust him? Would the feelings they'd once shared be enough to keep him from revealing facts that could ruin her?

Laurel couldn't be certain. Whatever he'd once felt for her may well have been destroyed by the bitterness that surrounded her leaving him. Still, she refused to panic. Alone, away from Sawyer and the long-dormant emotions he had stirred, the fresh air gradually cleared her head, permitting her usual logical self-composure to reassert itself. It occurred to her that all she really had to admit to Sawyer was that she had changed her name. That was a relatively minor—and no doubt common—form of deception.

There was no need for him to know the rest. No need for her to admit that although she'd worked hard, dedicated herself single-mindedly to her career, and earned each promotion along the way, it was all built on a lie. A lie that haunted Laurel, lurking always in the back of her mind, ready to pounce if she didn't keep busy enough to avoid thinking about it. A lie she would give anything to make right . . . anything, that is, except what it would cost her to do so: For it would cost her everything. Everything she had and was—and her promising future as well.

No, as much as she hated and regretted it, the lie would have to stand. As it was, it didn't really hurt anyone or anything . . . except her conscience. And she had learned to live with that. Just as she had learned to live without Sawyer.

"Dory?"

She spun around. There had been no sound of the French doors opening or closing, but obviously they had, because there was Sawyer, standing on the terrace behind her. Laurel had wanted to confront him privately, thinking it would be easier to face him alone. She'd been a fool. With the initial shock of seeing him past, and without the buffer of the others' presence, she was swept by the full impact of coming face to face with the only man she'd ever loved.

She suddenly realized that he didn't look exactly as she remembered or as she'd imagined so many times during the past eleven years. He looked better. His thick black hair, once a shoulder-length symbol of his refusal to conform, was much shorter and stylishly cut. And memory or imagination could never capture the magic in the way his seemingly ordinary features blended together—the square jaw and narrow nose he'd inherited from his father along with his six-foot-two height and broad shoulders, and the dark eyes and sensual mouth that Laurel had always romantically attributed to his mother's Mexican ancestry. He still looked like the football hero he'd been when they'd first met—a man's man and a woman's fantasy. If anything, the years had only enhanced the magnetic aura that surrounded him. Or maybe the years of abstinence had simply increased her susceptibility to him. Whichever, there was a distinctly warm feeling growing within her that made it very difficult to concentrate.

Now that they were alone, Sawyer's expression was starkly serious, with no trace of his earlier polite pretense, and Laurel warned herself to remember that, regardless of what he said or did, she could not afford the luxury of being totally honest with him.

"Dory," he said again, as if he needed some confirmation that it was really her.

Laurel straightened her back. "Don't call me that."

"Why not? It's your name, isn't it?"

"No. My name is Laurel."

"Oh, right. Laurel Forrest. Give me a break, Dory. That doesn't even sound like a name. It sounds like something you made up."

"You're only saying that because you happen to know it wasn't my given name."

"I'm saying it because it's true. Laurel Forrest." He shook his head, a small derisive smile curling his lips. "Why didn't you go all out and make it something really catchy like Emerald Forrest? Or better yet, National Forrest? I mean it, Dory. Anyone with an ounce of common sense could spot that name as a phony right off."

"Oh, really?" She smiled coolly. "Maybe that's true of people who think names like Billy-Bob are normal, but to anyone with any degree of sophistication it's a perfectly acceptable name. For instance, there's a whole roomful of people inside there who've never expressed the slightest doubt about Laurel Forrest being my real name."

"Which proves exactly nothing. Those people in there are all so busy playing their own games that if you said your name was Snow White, they'd smile and ask if the dwarfs have any connections on the Hill."

"More cynical than ever, I see."

"Maybe. Disillusionment has a way of doing that to a man."

Laurel struggled to appear unaffected by his hard stare. "Judging from appearances and what you were telling Marjorie a little while ago, I'd say you have little to be disillusioned about. I don't know how you went from running your father's store to offshore oil explorations, but I'm happy for you, Sawyer."

"Are you really, Dory?"

Her mouth tightened. "Please, I asked you not to call . . ."

"All right," he conceded, waving his hand impatiently. "I'll call you Laurel . . . for now. Are you really happy for me?"

"Of course." Her voice was soft. "I never wanted anything but the best for you, Sawyer."

"I'll go along with that, too . . . for now." His eyes burned, but it was an icy fire that made her uneasy. "Let's get more specific—are you happy to see me?"

She started to say, "Of course," then caught the words back. He would know that was a lie.

"Well?" Sawyer prodded, his harsh grin a challenge.

"Yes, I'm happy to see you," she replied carefully. "I just wish the circumstances were a little different."

"Different how?"

"I'm not sure. It's just that like this . . . things are . . . it's a little awkward."

"I'll bet. Tell me, what would happen if I went back in there right now and told all those people that your name isn't Laurel Forrest but Pandora Milinkus? And that the elite, society upbringing you've obviously told them about is as bogus as your name?"

Laurel felt a constricting pressure in her throat as she visualized the scene he described. "It would be very . . . embarrassing for me, naturally."

"Embarrassing? That's all?"

Laurel hesitated, choosing her words cautiously. "It would change some things, I suppose."

"Like the *thing* you have going with Jasper Dane?" Sawyer drawled, his smile becoming lazy and suggestive.

"It's not like that with Jasper."

His brows lifted. "Not like what?"

"Like what you're thinking."

"Why don't you tell me what I'm thinking?"

"Listen, I know how this must look to you . . ." Laurel shifted restlessly so that she was staring into the night instead of into the condemnation in Sawyer's dark eyes. "I mean, I changed my name, lied about my past, and now it's no secret that I . . . that Jasper and I . . . that we're close," she finished lamely. Why couldn't she come right out and say that in all likelihood she would soon be married to Jasper Dane?

"Just how close are you?"

"We're friends."

"As good friends as you and I used to be, Dory?" His soft tone made the question a slap in the face.

She spun back to face him, her green eyes flashing angrily. "That's none of your business."

He nodded. His expression was uncaring except for the telltale muscle that jumped on the left side of his mouth—just the way Laurel remembered it always had when he was quietly furious.

"Well, anyway, you can relax," he said after a moment. "Whatever your setup with Jasper is, I won't blow it—or anything else you've got cooking—by telling anyone who you really are."

Laurel's gaze slid to the flagstone beneath her feet. "Thank you."

"Don't thank me yet. There is one condition on my silence. I'll go along with your performance in public, but when we're alone I expect complete, total honesty between us." He hooked his thumb under her chin and tipped her face toward his. "Deal?"

It seemed to Laurel that she didn't have much choice at the moment but to smile and go along with him. "Deal."

Sawyer didn't buy her innocent smile or her sudden acquiescence, but he didn't press. At the moment he wasn't feeling up to a cat-and-mouse game of words. The fact was, he was still reeling from seeing her again this way. His brain felt slightly numb and the rest of his body felt like it was racing . . . trying to make up for eleven wasted years. God, she was more beautiful than ever. Her hair, her eyes, her body—everything about her was different and yet the same. She even felt the same, he realized, permitting his thumb to skate lightly across her skin, silky and wonderful. The soft familiarity of her might not be enough to wipe out all his anger and pain, but it certainly was cutting a wide swathe through it, touching him in ways and places he hadn't been touched in a long, long time.

Abruptly he dropped his hand back to his side.

"I'm glad you agree," he said without smiling. "Because I want to know everything that's happened to you since you left Beaumont, and I don't want to have to wonder if what you're telling me is as make-believe as your childhood in Seaside."

Laurel blushed. "I wouldn't lie to you like that." Unless I absolutely had to, she added silently. Please, God, let him not badger me for details. "There really isn't very much to tell," she began. "My life hasn't been anything like the success story yours has been. When I left—"

"Uh-uh, Dory . . . I mean, Laurel," he interrupted. "Not now and definitely not here. I don't want some hurried sketch of the high points of the last eleven years. I want to know everything . . . I want to know you, the way I used to know you. And that's going to take time. Have lunch with me tomorrow." He grinned. "Better yet, have breakfast with me so I don't have to wait so long to see you again."

"I can't," Laurel replied, even as excitement sizzled inside her. She hadn't thought past tonight, hadn't even considered that she might see him again. But now that the possibility had been raised, she found that she wanted to . . . very much. Despite the risks involved. "I have to work tomorrow," she explained.

Surprise flickered in his eyes.

"Does that surprise you, Sawyer?" she demanded, irritated. "Did you think I just sat around all day waiting for Jasper to come and visit me?"

"No, that's not what I thought." Actually, he was so overwhelmed to find her again that his thinking processes seemed to be progressing about as efficiently as a rowboat in the snow. A weakness he was no way going to admit to her. "Marjorie didn't mention anything about you having a job," he continued in what he hoped was a convincingly offhand manner, "and I guess I just didn't think about it. If I had, I would have realized you must work at something."

"I work at 'something' all right," countered Laurel, mimicking his condescending tone. "And the something I work at is the State Department, as a special assistant in the Office of Protocol. And before you do anymore thinking about it, let me tell you . . . it's no patronage job. I got it on my own, and I work damn hard at it."

"I'm sure you do. If I jumped to conclusions about you and Dane, I'm sorry." And relieved as hell, he thought but didn't say out loud. "It's obvious you've made quite a life for yourself. It looks like you have everything you always wanted—success, excitement, respect . . . as well as one thing you've always had." He dropped his voice and let his eyes touch her in all the places his hands burned to. "You're more beautiful than ever, Dory."

This time she didn't protest his use of the old nickname, the one only he had ever called her. She was too busy trying to control the feelings of excitement that his husky compliment and heated gaze had unleashed inside her. He was standing close—too close, really—his head angled slightly toward her. His warm breath brushed her cheek, alerting her to the fact that he was breathing just as shallowly and rapidly as she was. His mere closeness made all the tiny hairs on her arms rise with a sort of tingling sensation. Laurel knew that if the silence continued even one more second, his mouth would lower and open over hers, and then she would be lost.

"I guess we've both been lucky," she said in a rushed, unnatural-sounding voice. "We've had more than our share of success in getting what we wanted out of life."

That she of all people could suggest that he had even remotely gotten what he wanted out of life made Sawyer laugh harshly. "Not me. I have a lot of things now, all the things I wanted to give to you, all the things I used to promise you. But the one thing I wanted most I don't have."

Laurel knew what was coming and started to turn away. He stopped her by catching her arm in an unyielding grip.

"Do you know what that one thing is, Laurel Forrest?"

"I don't think we should discuss this, Sawyer. It's
been a long time and . . ."

"A very long time. Eleven years. After I got over
being furious with you for leaving me, I tried to find
you and guess what? There was no trace of a Pandora
Milinkus anywhere. It was just like you'd dropped off
the face of the earth. At first that was the driving reason
for me to make money . . . to keep on paying for detec-
tives to tell me it was a lost cause. Then I convinced
myself that someday you'd come back on your own,
and when you did I was determined to be the richest
man in Beaumont just so I could rub your nose in it."

Sawyer knew he was rambling, saying things that
might best be left unsaid, but dammit, he had a right.
He'd waited a long time to say these things to this
woman and she was damn well going to hear them. "I
worked compulsively to build up the company. I bought
cars and built houses just to flaunt them in front of you
when you finally came back. I was going to show you
that I could buy all the things that I didn't have before
you left me . . . the trappings of success that were so important to you."

The pain that ripped through Laurel was every bit as
sharp as it had been the last time they'd argued about
this very subject. That had been eleven years ago, sitting in Sawyer's car on the old Post Road. Then their
argument had ended with Sawyer lying on top of her,
coming closer than she had ever thought he could to
taking her by force. Judging from the look on his face
now and the emotions churning inside her, time had
done little to temper either of their feelings on this subject.

"That's not why I left, Sawyer," she said, her very
tone a plea for him to understand. "You know that."

"Wrong. I know that's exactly why you left."

Laurel cringed at his tone. It was cold, condemning, that of a man whose mind had been made up long ago. "You never understood—"

"Of course I understood," Sawyer broke in, his anger surging along a well-worn path. "You made it very clear. Beaumont was a small town and you had big plans . . . too big to include the son of a shopkeeper."

"That's a rotten lie." Tearing her arm free from his hold, she whirled to face him head on. "Yes, I had plans, and yes, I hated Beaumont, Texas, and everything it symbolized to me. I wanted to get away. I wanted to be somebody . . . anybody other than poor Pandora Milinkus. You of all people knew that. You knew I didn't want to end up like my sisters—married, with a passel of kids and nothing to look forward to but a weekly night out to play bingo."

"It wouldn't have been like that for us," Sawyer protested, feeling ridiculously injured by her attitude about something that had happened a lifetime ago. "I promised you that."

"Promises can be broken."

He felt stunned, then furious at the implication in those few quiet words. The air between them hummed as anger and pain long held on simmer bubbled to the surface.

"I'm sorry if that hurts you," Laurel said hurriedly, before he could lash out at her, "but it's the truth. I loved you, Sawyer, but I was too scared to risk trading my future for a bunch of promises."

"So instead, you left me, walked away and never looked back?"

"God, no." She shivered, and tears welled up behind her eyelids. "If looking back means remembering and missing someone and wishing you could see them, touch them, for just a minute to make the hurting stop, then I looked over my shoulder for . . . a long, long time," she concluded, unwilling to reveal to him exactly how long. The truth was she'd never stopped remembering.

"It was within your power to see me, touch me, if that's what you really wanted," he pointed out. "You could have come home."

"And you could have come with me," she cried, forgetting for a second that only a screen of shrubs separated them from whomever might be on the adjacent terrace. When she spoke again her voice was lower but still anguished. "That was another promise you made me, remember? That as soon as I turned eighteen we would leave. We were supposed to get married, Sawyer . . . how do you think I felt? Yes, I had big plans, but every one of them included you. It was *you,* not me, who changed his mind."

"Because I had no other choice," he shot back. Inside, he felt that old sense of frustration pressing in on him. Frustration because he couldn't take her or fate in his hands and make them into what he wanted them to be; frustration because some tiny, clear-seeing part of him suspected that she may be right, might have been right all along. "And at least get it straight," he growled, overriding that tiny voice inside. "I didn't change my mind. I just asked you to wait a while."

"Exactly how long is a *while,* Sawyer? Eleven years ago you couldn't answer that question for me. Did you ever figure it out?"

"I gave you an answer . . . however long it took for me to take care of things." His jaw clenched as he glared down at her. "What the hell did you expect me to do, Dory? When we made our plans to leave, I didn't count on my father having a heart attack . . . I didn't count on him dying so inconveniently. Did you think I wanted to stand behind a counter and sell fishing tackle instead of taking off with you? I didn't. But I didn't have any choice. I had to think of my mother and Pete," he said, referring to his younger brother.

"Without me," he continued, "they wouldn't have had half a chance of keeping the store going. All I wanted was for you to wait until I could figure out some way to make sure they were taken care of." He shook his head with such bitterness that Laurel had to fight not to cringe. "But that was asking too much of you ... after all, you had *plans*."

"That's not fair ... you're making my decision to leave sound selfish and calculating."

"Wasn't it?"

"No. It was a matter of survival."

He gave a short, harsh laugh.

"It's true, Sawyer," she insisted. "I couldn't have survived if I'd stayed in Beaumont. Part of me would have died there. You know what it was like for me."

"It would have been different after we were married."

"Not different enough," Laurel stated firmly. "Contrary to what you might have heard, love doesn't conquer all."

"How the hell would you know? You never even gave it a chance."

"First, I had to give me a chance, dammit. I was so young. Maybe I didn't handle it as well as I should have, but I was afraid all our dreams and plans would just gradually slip away." Her chin lifted stubbornly. "Love has to involve freedom. It shouldn't mean having to give up everything else you ever wanted."

"Love also involves responsibility, and that's something you obviously couldn't handle. Maybe you still can't ... maybe that's why you prance around with a phony name, making up stories about where you come from. Maybe you're just as selfish and immature now as you were the day you ran away from me."

"And you're just as thick-headed on the subject," Laurel shot back, cursing the heat that flooded her cheeks in response to his angry taunts.

"No. I'm even worse. I've had a good long time to stew about it. Only now I don't take no for an answer as easily as I did then."

"You never took it easily," she murmured, but it was as if he didn't hear. His gaze held hers prisoner as he lifted his hands to her face, cradling her delicate chin and flushed cheeks with his strong, narrow fingers.

"You see, I've also had a lot of time to learn how to get what I want . . . everything I want," he added, leaning even closer. "You'd do well to remember that, *Laurel*. I've had to work and scrape and fight for everything I've ever wanted, but in the end, I always get it."

Then his mouth came down hard to claim hers.

After the initial surprise, the warm pressure of his lips and sure, firm thrust of his tongue were like a ride back through time. Laurel responded to him with a passion that was pure instinct, and her head sang with the sheer rightness of it. These were the lips that could set her world on fire. These were the arms that had the power to make her feel safe and protected. This kiss, this passion, this man. Sawyer. She'd been running from him and looking for him for years.

Without thinking, she let her body relax against his, discovering that all the soft curves and sharp planes meshed as perfectly as they ever had. She inhaled the clean, fresh scent of soap and man that was heavenly familiar. It brought back a vivid memory of hours spent parked in his car at the beach, hours snatched before school or right afterward because it was the only time they could be together. Laurel rode the memory, and her mouth opened hungrily under his.

Sawyer felt the sweet invitation of her lips parting for him and knew kissing her had been a mistake . . . probably about the hundredth he'd made tonight. He usually considered any kiss undertaken in a vertical position to be a preliminary test of sorts to see how receptive a woman was to moving on to more interesting activity. Now, however, as she slowly slid her tongue over his lips, he realized this might well be more activity than he could handle in such a public place. Kissing her was like handing a jug of cold water to a man in the desert and telling him to take only one small sip. Sawyer wasn't sure he could be so self-controlled, wasn't sure he even wanted to try.

The soft, hungry sound that rippled from her throat sent a tremor through his body, and deep inside he felt a tidal wave of desire begin to build. Raw, primitive desire—not the kind that played coy games or heeded the boundaries of socially acceptable behavior. Recklessly, he deepened the kiss, greedy for the sweet, moist taste of her that for so long had been only a memory, a teasing shadow in his dreams. Just a few seconds more, he told himself, knowing he was tempting fate with each instant their bodies and mouths remained fused. Already he was dangerously close to claiming what was his then and there, and Jasper Dane and the rest of the Washington socialites inside be damned.

Laurel's hands curled over his shoulders as his fingers caressed the bare skin of her back above the dress's dipping neckline. The feel of her was driving him crazy. He wanted to slide his hands around to the front of her dress—to feel her breasts and the nipples he knew must be already hard. Actually, he wanted to do a hell of a lot more than that, and, after escalating the kiss to a surge of erotic thrusts, that fearful knowledge gave him the strength to end it abruptly, lifting his head and leaving her draped over his arm in bewilderment.

"Tomorrow," he whispered, his voice husky, revealing a degree of emotion he would have preferred to keep hidden. "Breakfast."

The words were a command, a promise, a challenge. Still dizzy from kissing him, Laurel shook her head automatically. "No."

"Yes. We have unfinished business, you and I."

He grinned as he said it, and full awareness returned to her in a shot. With it came a wretched feeling of humiliation. Straightening, she took a long step backward, away from him. She moved awkwardly, to the tune of his amused chuckle.

"No, Sawyer," she said with as much dignity as she could muster. "I'm afraid that whatever we once had is quite finished."

He squinted at her in disbelief. "Do you really believe that?"

"Of course."

"Then I guess I didn't do as good a job as I thought of showing you otherwise. Come back here." He reached for her, but Laurel took another lurching step backward.

"Don't you dare touch me. I'm not seventeen years old anymore . . . and I don't make a practice of groping at parties."

"Really? You could have fooled me the way you fell into it so naturally a few minutes ago."

"You're . . ."—she shook her head—"impossible. Please, can't you just wipe the slate clean and leave me alone . . . if only for old time's sake?"

"For old time's sake." He repeated the words slowly, as if savoring them. "If it makes you feel better, Laurel, old pal, I plan to do a great deal to you for *old time's sake* . . . but leaving you alone isn't part of it."

Laurel smoothed her dress, taking pains not to let him see the uneasiness his words incited inside her. "Well, you can't do much without my cooperation, and you can forget about ever getting that."

"I'm willing to take my chances," he drawled, a smile slowly lifting the corners of his wide mouth.

"Fine, but you'll lose. Just don't forget that you gave me your word not to say anything to anyone about what you know about me."

"And don't forget your part of the deal . . . total honesty when we're alone together."

"Oh, I won't forget," Laurel assured him, unable to suppress a triumphant smile as she turned away. "But I intend to see to it that we're not alone together again."

"Good luck."

His unbridled laugh followed her as she opened the door and walked quickly through Marjorie's sitting room. She didn't intend to rely on luck, good or otherwise, to avoid Sawyer. She would handle it the same way she did everything else, with intelligence and determination. He would only be in town a week; surely she could manage to be excruciatingly busy and absolutely unavailable for that long.

Jasper was waiting for her just inside the living room, his expression anxious. "Laurel? Are you all right? I was beginning to worry."

"I'm fine, Jasper. I ran into Mr. Gates in the hallway, and it turns out we do have a few acquaintances in common, after all." Laurel was a firm believer in always sticking as close to the truth as circumstances permitted.

"I'm glad to hear that," Jasper countered. "It seems that Riordon planned to spend the next few days showing his friend Gates around Washington, but something has come up in the Senate and he'll be tied up there. Seeing as how you and Gates share a home state, I thought it would be neighborly of you to offer to fill in as tour guide." That it was also a golden opportunity to dispense a little propaganda in Jasper's behalf went unspoken.

Laurel smiled, the wheels in her head spinning in a frantic search for an escape route. "Jasper, you know I would love to help out, but I'm afraid this is a busy week at the office for me as well. We still have a million details to take care of for the prime minister's visit, and I haven't even touched base yet with the team handling security. On top of that, I have a new intern starting tomorrow. Perhaps later in the week," she trailed off vaguely.

"No, that won't do at all." A fan of deep grooves appeared between Jasper's lowered brows. "Maybe if we spoke to Bill, he could help you to free up some time."

Laurel's teeth clenched as he turned to rake the crowd with a determined gaze. He was searching, she knew, for her boss and his good friend Bill Reynolds. There was little doubt that Bill would approve of her taking days, weeks, even months off from work if it would help Jasper's cause. In an avalanche of bad luck, Jasper spotted Bill standing in a group to their left and reached out to tap his arm just as Sawyer and Senator Riordon closed in on her from the right.

Exactly as she'd feared, upon hearing Jasper's explanation of the situation, Bill quickly agreed to arrange coverage for Laurel at the office, encouraging her in a loud, jovial tone to take as much time off as she needed. Laurel couldn't ask for a better boss, but at that moment nothing would have given her more pleasure than to smother the man with the cream puff cradled in his hand. Wearing a frozen smile, she casually glanced Sawyer's way to check out his reaction to her bad fortune. It was also as she expected: smug.

"It looks like our problem is solved," Mike Riordon said, slapping Sawyer's shoulder. "Thanks for coming to my rescue, Laurel. I'm sure Sawyer will find you're a better guide than I am and a whole lot more pleasant to look at."

"I'm happy to help," Laurel lied. "But I wonder if Mr. Gates wouldn't be more comfortable with someone from your own staff, Senator." At best, it was a feeble escape attempt, but she wasn't about to go down without a fight.

"My name's Sawyer," he reminded her before Riordon could speak. "And I'm sure no one could make me feel more welcome than a fellow Texan."

"Well, then, it's all settled," announced Jasper with an enthusiasm Laurel suddenly found irritating.

Plucking two crystal tulip glasses of champagne from the tray of a passing waiter, Sawyer held one in front of Laurel until she was forced to accept it.

"To an early start tomorrow," he drawled, lifting his glass and pointedly waiting for her to do likewise.

Laurel tightened her lips into a smile, murmuring something she hoped was sufficiently gracious as she reluctantly followed suit. Their glasses touched in mid-air with a click that sounded as ominous to her as the door of a lion's den swinging shut behind her.

Chapter Three

"ALL RIGHT, WHAT would you like me to show you first?" Laurel purposely let her tone reflect the fact that she was there under duress.

Above the gold-plated rim of his coffee cup, Sawyer's mouth twisted into a suggestive grin. "Do you really want me to answer that?"

"No," she snapped. "What I really want is not to have to spend the rest of the day playing this adolescent game of double-entendre with you."

"Too bad. For some reason just the sight of you jerks me back to those glandular days of adolescence." Although his smile lingered, the humor washed from his eyes. "It's like I told you last night, Laurel, there's unfinished business between us."

The nature of that unfinished business had kept Laurel awake most of the night. With a disdainful sigh, she averted her eyes from the challenge in his and feigned great interest in the early morning activity outside on Massachusetts Avenue. They were sitting at a window table in the Jockey Club at the Ritz-Carlton. On principal, Laurel would have preferred to meet on more neutral terrority than Sawyer's hotel. But last evening, with Jasper and Mike Riordon as eager spectators, she'd had no choice but to acquiesce gracefully when he'd insisted they plan the day's agenda over an early breakfast.

Now, an hour and a half after they'd been seated, he'd polished off a warrior-sized meal of ham and eggs and was dawdling over his third cup of coffee while her bowl of raspberries and cream still sat, barely touched. Even as Laurel pushed aside thoughts of what her lack of appetite revealed about the state of her nerves, Sawyer's bright gaze zeroed in on the bowl.

"Not hungry this morning?" he inquired, cynicism underlying his light tone.

"Not very."

"Another thing that's changed about you. I remember when you had a ravenous appetite early in the morning. But then, maybe your mornings were more . . . activity-filled back in those days."

Laurel suspected there was a question about her relationship with Jasper buried somewhere in that remark, but it wasn't one she cared to answer. She sipped her lukewarm coffee in silence.

Resting an elbow on the starched linen tablecloth, Sawyer leaned toward her. "We used to buy chocolate frosted donuts at Allie's and drive out to the beach. Between us, we'd polish off a whole dozen. Remember?"

She did, achingly.

"No," she replied.

"I do. I also remember drinking from the same carton of milk because we forgot to bring paper cups. And I remember licking the traces of chocolate frosting from the corners of your mouth, and how then we'd suddenly forget all about the donuts until we found them crushed beneath one of us a long time later."

Laurel closed her eyes to the storm of emotion in his, but there was no way she could escape the rasp of his voice.

"Most of all, though," he went on, "I remember always pulling back, always stopping short until I was so frustrated that whole days . . . weeks . . . would go by when it seemed like I thought of nothing but having you. But I waited, because that was the way you wanted it. I've been waiting a long time."

At that moment he seemed to be waiting for her to say something, to acknowledge something. Laurel forced herself to look at him, to face the anger and pain in his tight-lipped expression.

"I'm sorry." It was ludicrous, totally insufficient, but it was all she could think of to say. Against the crisp, white linen of her trousers her hands twisted restlessly. "That was all a long time ago."

Sawyer nodded. "That's what I kept telling myself whenever some stupid memory would crop up. Like the way your nose freckled in the sun or how small your hand always felt in mine. I'd push it away and tell myself that all that was part of a time long past, a time that couldn't possibly have been as special or perfect as it is in my fantasies. And I told myself that whatever it was, it was over. It almost felt that way, too. Until last night. Last night changed everything."

Afraid to meet the intensity of his eyes, Laurel dropped her gaze to the table only to find a different sort of danger waiting there. The sight of Sawyer's hand, so brown against the snowy white tablecloth, uprooted even more carefully buried memories. She'd always loved his hands, thought their shape and rough texture intrinsically male and very sexy. His palm was broad, his fingers long and lean and blunt tipped. Those agile fingers had caressed her hundreds, maybe thousands of

times. They had touched and explored each curve and
hollow of her body, learning her most intimate secrets
—and teaching them to her. His fingers had stroked her,
gently, roughly. . .

"More coffee?"

The cheerful voice of the waiter made her jump.

"Not for me, thanks," Sawyer replied. "Laurel?"

"No . . . thank you." Quickly regaining her composure, she added, "In fact, I really think we should be
leaving. You do want to get in some sightseeing today,
don't you?"

"Not especially," he countered with a shrug.

Somehow that didn't come as a total surprise.

"Regardless, as long as that's the supposed purpose
for this farce, I plan to do my part. So let's try again;
what would you like to see first?"

Lounging back in his chair, Sawyer unleashed a lazy
smile. "Surprise me. No, really," he added quickly
when Laurel rolled her eyes and tossed her napkin impatiently onto the table. "You're the native here; show
me your city."

Laurel paused, thinking. This tour guide role was a
new one for her. She'd never before been presented with
family members or old friends for whom to show off her
adopted city. Given a free rein, she found herself rapidly
warming to the prospect.

"I suppose the obvious place to start would be the
White House . . . or maybe the Washington Monument."
She glanced at her watch. "Of course, the Smithsonian
is less crowded early. . ."

"Hold it."

She glanced up, surprised to find Sawyer shaking his
head.

"I'm not interested in any of that," he announced.

"Any of *that?*" echoed Laurel. *"That* just happens to
be your heritage—what everyone who comes to Washington wants to see."

He shrugged. "I'm not like everyone else."

"No kidding."

His response to her muttering was a grin that carved deep lines at the corners of his eyes, lines that hadn't been there eleven years ago. For some reason the sight of them stabbed Laurel with a sudden sharp, painful image of a large chunk of her life that was gone, lost to her forever.

"Besides," he went on, "I can pick up postcards of those places in the hotel gift shop and learn more than I ever wanted to know about them from reading the backs. What I can't learn from a postcard is what it is about this city that keeps you here. And for the next week that's all I care about, getting to know you all over again."

The quiet determination in his voice as he implied today would not be the end of this unplanned reunion excited Laurel. And frightened her.

"What about the business that brought you here in the first place?" she asked, certain he was not really free to while away the rest of the week tormenting her.

"Business is business," he countered matter-of-factly. "It will either work out or it won't. Either way it's not something that will haunt me for the next eleven years of my life."

Once more Laurel saw that quick, dark flash of anger in his eyes. Then it was gone and he was smiling at her, a familiar, beguiling smile that she found herself responding to without thinking.

"So what's it going to be?" he asked, scribbling his signature on the check the waiter brought.

"I don't know. I'm not quite sure what you expect me to show you if not the traditional tourist sights."

"Show me how you spend your time when you're not working. What do you do on your day off?"

"Laundry."

"Perfect. Take me to your local laundromat. I can't

think of a faster way of getting to know a woman than helping to sort her dirty clothes."

Laurel rested her chin in her hand, laughing at his enthusiastic leer. "Out of the question. I'm not having you report back to Mike Riordon that the highlight of your tour of the city was my wash."

"Mike Riordon has nothing to do with this, Laurel," Sawyer quickly informed her in a gravelly voice. "And neither does Jasper Dane. This is strictly between you and me."

"Still," she countered, wishing everything he said didn't have that momentous edge that sent shivers up her spine, "I am not taking you to a laundromat."

He settled back in his chair. "And I'm not letting you take me to the Washington Monument. Should I order us some more coffee?"

Laurel's frown barely had time to get started before it was chased from her face by a smug smile. A gleam of anticipation lit her eyes.

"No, don't bother," she replied. "I think I know of something we can do. It's something that would fascinate the Sawyer Gates I used to know, and I have a hunch you haven't changed all that much."

"Shark feeding?" Sawyer's expression was satisfyingly confused. She had refused to tell him where they were headed as they walked the short distance to the National Aquarium. She'd kept her fingers crossed the whole way that they wouldn't be too late for the public feeding demonstration, and they weren't. Seated on one of the benches that circled the basement tank, waiting for the show to start, Laurel struggled to untangle the impulse that had prompted her to bring him here of all places.

"This is really one of your favorite places?" he pressed.

"I've never thought of it in that way, but actually," she said with a sheepish nod, "yes, it is."

He appeared interested. No, more than interested, Laurel decided, fascinated.

"Why, for God's sake?" he asked.

"Just look at them." She nodded toward the tank where several dark shadows circled underwater, their shiny blue-gray fins slicing the smooth surface. "They're so totally competent at what they do. No wasted motion, no wrong paths chosen—and they're even more so once the food's dumped in. Then they're relentless, aggressive, setting their sights on their goal and closing in on it with no second thoughts, no doubts about whether they're right or wrong or what the consequences might be."

"Offhand, I'd say you're a little like that yourself."

The casually voiced remark brought Laurel's head around sharply. "Me?"

Sawyer nodded. "You left Beaumont with a goal—to be a success—and you've certainly succeeded."

"Oh, I can set goals, all right," Laurel agreed, "but there are always doubts, always second thoughts getting in the way."

"What kind of doubts?"

Immediately she swung her gaze back to the tank and clamped shut the small gate in her mind that had begun to inch open as she relaxed. She couldn't afford to relax, couldn't afford to let the distant familiarity of being with Sawyer lull her into forgetting what was at risk. But it was going to be a battle. Already she found herself slipping back into a comfortable pattern of closeness, and the more time they spent together the worse it was bound to get.

"Doubts too foolish to waste time talking about," she said crisply in response to his question. To keep the conversational spotlight off of her, she slanted him a measuring glance. "Actually, of the two of us, I'd say you're the more sharklike. How *did* you manage to become a tycoon at the tender age of thirty-two?"

He gave a short laugh that sounded blatantly self-deprecatory. "By accident . . . and the term tycoon hardly applies. I have two partners and a lot of wealth on paper. I'm never sure when I go to bed at night that it will all be there come morning. Oil exploration is a risky business. It makes professional gambling look like a sure thing by comparison."

"What was the accident part of it?"

"When I first started running the store I was so angry—at you for leaving me and at my father for dying and sticking me behind the counter of a marine supply store when all I wanted was to take off after you—that I guess I subconsciously decided to do everything he wouldn't want done. He never extended credit to anyone, so I did, letting anyone run up a bill who asked for it. Bad risks, good risks, I didn't quibble. Maybe deep down I wanted to go bust so I'd be free."

"But you didn't."

"No, I didn't . . . although I came damn close," he admitted with a quickly fleeing smile. "One of those bad risks I extended credit to was a guy named Dak . . . Stanley Dakin. He ran a small supply boat that serviced offshore oil rigs."

Laurel peered at him questioningly.

"Ferrying out food supplies and equipment to the rigs," he explained, "and taxiing the crews back and forth. The big oil companies are glad to pay for the service so they don't have to maintain a boat and a full-time crew to handle it. Managed well, it can be a very lucrative business."

"Was this Dak a good manager?"

Sawyer shook his head, wincing. "Miserable. He was in debt to me within a few months for more than his boat was worth. I knew that even if he sold it and turned the cash over to me, I'd be losing out. So instead, I took half ownership in the boat and Dakin Offshore Services and demanded a full vote in its operation."

"And?" Laurel prodded.

"And no one was more surprised than Dak and me when it started to show a profit." He leaned back, resting his elbows on the bench above theirs and stretching his long, denim-clad legs out in front. "When one of the small-time rig operators we serviced ran into some financial troubles a couple of years later, we'd grown big enough to buy into his operation and supply the capital needed to turn it around. That's when we picked up our third partner, Reece Andrews, and wound up in the oil exploration business."

"So now the three of you jointly run all three businesses?"

"Not exactly. Dak was killed in a boating accident a few years ago," he told her. His voice was low, and Laurel knew without asking that the two men had been good friends as well as business partners.

"I'm sorry, Sawyer."

"Yeah. Well . . ." He kept his eyes focused on the sharks for a few seconds before turning back to her. "His wife, Maureen, took over his share, and she's damn good at it. A real crackerjack. She keeps Reece and me hustling. As a matter of fact, it's a project she originated with some oil leases in the North Sea that's my reason for being here." His expression heated into an intense, smoky look that Laurel felt all the way to her toes. "I'll have to remember to thank Maureen."

Her own eyes huge and slightly bewildered, Laurel searched the emotion-riddled depths of his, trying to see what exactly was there. What did he have to thank Maureen for? Throwing her into his path again after eleven years? And what did he want with her anyway? To take up where they'd left off? Or to punish her for what he saw as an act of betrayal? From moment to moment, Laurel wasn't sure. His mood could swing from teasingly seductive to tightly reined anger and back again so quickly it was hard to know what he was really thinking.

Like now. The look of sensual awareness that had heated every inch of her flesh had disappeared, and he was regarding her with a bemused half smile, no doubt delighted with himself for having rendered her tongue-tied and doe-eyed.

"Look," he instructed, pointing to the trainer who'd just arrived toting an overflowing bucket of fish. "Lunch is about to be served. Pay attention, and you might pick up some pointers."

He leaned closer. The warmth of his breath on her face left Laurel feeling a little dazed, so it was a few seconds before the implication of his next words penetrated.

"I'm beginning to realize," he told her in a self-satisfied purr of a voice, "that you haven't done as great a job of getting what you really want out of life as I first thought."

"Now this is more like it," Sawyer pronounced. "I can easily understand this being one of your favorite places."

They were standing outside a monstrous cage at the National Zoological Park, watching the two giant, black-and-white pandas frolicking inside. For the last hour or so they'd wandered around the scenic park, munching hot dogs and lingering at the exhibits of gorillas and white Bengal tigers. As the day went on, more and more fragments of memories from the past worked their way to the surface, triggered by the sight of a balloon vendor or the smell of cotton candy, making it increasingly difficult for him to keep Laurel at an emotional distance. Something he was determined to do.

But no matter how he tried to ignore them, the ties

from the past were still there, unavoidable and even, strangely, feeling as strong as ever once the cobwebs were blown away. Without warning, the most casual, superficial remark could trigger an emotional chain reaction that left the air between them vibrating. And each time it happened Sawyer resolved to pick his words more carefully from then on. Not that he had any objections to their relationship vibrating—in fact, he was planning on exactly that. What he didn't want was to feel anything beyond those physical vibrations...no tenderness, no concern, nothing resembling what he'd been fool enough to feel for her once before.

"You're right," Laurel said, confirming his observation about the zoo being one of her favorite places. "I do like it here."

"I can tell. You look like you want to reach right in and scoop up one of the pandas to cuddle." For the past five minutes he'd been watching her watch the bears, entranced by the sheer joy in her expression. It occurred to him that this was the first time he'd seen her look anywhere near that happy or unguarded. "I guess they bring out all your deep-seated maternal instincts, huh?"

Laurel regarded him with raised brows. "It has been a long time if you've confused me with someone who has strong maternal instincts."

"Oh, you have them, all right," he assured her, at the same time assuring himself that he wasn't irked by her smug attitude. "You always have had those instincts. You just harbor this crazy notion that they're a sign of weakness, so you keep them tightly under wraps."

"I harbor no such idea," Laurel informed him with another one of those small, dismissive smiles she seemed to have spent the past eleven years perfecting.

"No? Then why haven't you ever had any?" Sawyer tried hard not to sound triumphant. He'd been waiting all day for an opening like this one. This was just the tip of the iceberg of things he wanted to know about her.

"Any what?"

"Kids."

"In case you didn't notice, I'm not married."

"I noticed all right. I just didn't know marriage was a prerequisite for getting pregnant."

Laurel decided to ignore him and pretended to be absorbed by the antics of one panda enthusiastically splashing water on the other. Naturally, it was the male doing the splashing. Bear or man, there was something in that Y-chromosome that compelled them to tease and taunt and stir the waters of a perfect, peaceful afternoon.

"So, why didn't you?" Sawyer prodded after her lengthening silence convinced him that she wasn't going to continue the conversation voluntarily.

"Why didn't I wh—"

Enough was enough. "Get married," he broke in brusquely. "So you could get pregnant. Have kids. Add to the world population problem."

"That's why," she shot back. "I'm a gung-ho member of that zero population group . . . what's it called?" Now he was the one watching the bears with a stone-jawed expression. "Well, whatever it's called, that's me."

They both leaned on the wrought-iron outer fence and fixed their eyes on the cage; six inches of very silent, very tension-filled space between them. Sawyer was determined that night could fall—hell, *snow* could fall—before he begged her for information. He had other ways of finding out, and he wasn't above using them.

"Oh, all right," Laurel finally gave in. "I guess the truth is that marriage and kids just never fit into my lifestyle."

Sawyer smiled, and realized ruefully that it was a smile sparked by relief. He hadn't wanted to hear that there had been someone important in her life since him, someone she'd considered having babies with. He couldn't help having a male ego. "At least now you're honoring your promise to be honest," he noted generously.

"So I am." She swung around to glare at his profile, evidently not impressed by his noble compliment. "And as long as you raised the subject, why didn't *you* ever get married and have kids?"

Sawyer bit back an automatic response and instead turned to her with a mocking smile. "What makes you so sure I didn't?"

Of course, Sawyer would have married. That obvious truth hit Laurel with all the subtlety of the Aisan flu and left her feeling just as weak. For all his maverick aloofness, she had always known that what Sawyer really wanted—needed—out of life was the kind of close, loving family neither of them had been blessed with.

From the instant they'd met, when he'd come barreling through the school parking lot in his much envied Chevy convertible and frightened her into losing her footing and landing rump first on the blacktop, he'd never tried to hide the compassionate side of his nature. That day he'd picked her up, brushed her off, and insisted on driving her home to the ramshackle, rented house she was mortified to have him see. It might have been the Taj Mahal for all that Sawyer appeared to notice. He had courteously walked her to the front door, smoothly and without comment avoiding the broken porch step and unhinged screen door, carefully protecting her dignity. That's the way he was. Intuitively knowing what someone needed and giving it. Perfect husband and father material.

Only now that thought filled Laurel not with tenderness, but with heartache. How could she ever have left him? Suddenly it was hard to call to mind all the old reasons and all she'd attained in exchange for a life with Sawyer. Instead, her head was crowded with images of a woman she didn't even know, Sawyer's wife. At this very moment she was probably home in Beaumont, clad in a French bikini as she lounged by a pool bought with Sawyer's sweat and determination. Shadowy figures of children hovered at the edges of her mind as well, dark haired and dark eyed. Laughing children, secure in a happy, loving home. She felt like throwing up.

"You can unclench your teeth." Sawyer's disparaging tone pierced her self-imposed misery. "I've never been married and I don't have any kids."

After checking his eyes to make sure he was honoring their agreement to be honest, Laurel lifted one shoulder in a negligent shrug. "As if it could possibly make any difference to me."

"Is that so?" he asked, gloating shamelessly. Her stricken reaction to his teasing had filled him with a ridiculous sense of elation. He didn't want to ask himself why he cared that she cared about his marital status. "Then how come you suddenly went so white I can count the freckles on your nose from here?"

"I did no such thing."

"Oh, no? One, two, three . . ."

"Oh, stop. So I was taken a little by surprise. Your marital status is really of no concern to me."

"Sure."

Silence.

"I do wonder, though . . . just out of curiosity, of course . . ."

"Of course."

"Why *haven't* you ever married?"

"The standard reason—I never found the right woman."

She loved it.

"Oh, come on now. Even in Texas successful, good-looking—if somewhat thick-headed—men are hard to come by. I can't believe you weren't snatched up long ago." It was sneaky and self-serving, but Laurel wanted to hear more. She wanted to hear that after her, other women paled in comparison.

"Oh, there have been willing women, all right," Sawyer admitted, his mouth quirking as he remembered the quantity and variety of females who littered his past. "Some really fine women . . . just none with whom I particularly cared to spend the rest of my life."

Then they couldn't have been all that fine, Laurel thought smugly, but wisely refrained from saying so.

"I would like to have kids, though," he continued. "But I firmly believe that before you have them, you ought to be prepared to provide them with what they need to be happy."

"I'd say you have the means to do that."

"I'm not talking about money."

"Neither am I," she said softly.

He stared at her, at first surprised and wary, waiting for the punch line. Gradually, he realized there wasn't going to be one, that she was being honest. He wasn't sure what to say to that. The silence lasted only a few seconds, but it rolled back the years and held them in a spell as unique and comforting as a favorite old robe. When Sawyer finally cleared his throat and looked around, he was a little stunned to find they were actually still standing in the middle of a crowd of laughing, jostling zoo-goers. A quick glance at Laurel told him that she was feeling just as out of place.

"C'mon," he said, grabbing her hand and pulling her through the throng. "Let's walk."

They made their way back to the flower-bordered path without speaking, their hands still linked. It felt right somehow. Sawyer knew it was crazy to feel so good about something as stupid as holding hands. But he did, and it bothered him that it did. He didn't know with whom he was more irritated, himself for feeling this way or her for saying things that made him second guess what he knew was the cold, bitter truth about her.

Just on principle he should probably be dropping her
hand as if it were a live wire. But he didn't, telling
himself she'd pull away soon enough on her own.

Laurel held her hand absolutely still in his, afraid
that if she moved, her nervousness would translate into
a sweaty palm. Oh, how he'd laugh at that. When they
reached the bend in the path, she promised herself, she
would pull free. But she didn't. Then she told herself
she would do it when they passed the popcorn stand.
The zebra cage. When he started to speak.

"Thanks for the vote of confidence back there," he
said finally, and Laurel, trying to remember what he
was thanking her for, completely forgot her latest promise to herself. "But you happen to be dead wrong."

"Wrong? Oh, you mean about kids and—"

"Right," he interrupted. "I don't come close to having what it takes to be a good father."

Without thinking, her fingers curled tighter around
his. "Sawyer..."

"I know I could give my kids fancy toys and the best
education money can buy." He went on as if he hadn't
heard her attempt to defend him from himself. "And
God knows I'd love them. But kids need more than that
to get them over the rough spots. They have a right to
more. They have a right to emotional support—the kind
that comes from being part of a family—and they have
a right to believe that it's going to be there for them
forever."

Laurel felt eminently unqualified to speak to this man
about emotional support. Especially now. All the
warmth that had gleamed in his eyes when he looked at
her just a few moments ago was suddenly gone, shut-
tered behind a gaze of blue-black ice. "That's one good
thing that came out of your running away from me. It
taught me my limitations. Lady, I'll never believe in
forever again."

* * *

The very last thing Laurel felt like doing after they'd left the zoo was battling the crowd on the metro to reach the National Geographic Society. She felt physically exhausted and emotionally battered. Unfortunately, when she suggested calling it a day, Sawyer, the king of postcard sightseeing, suddenly developed a burning desire to see for himself the society's mammoth globe she'd so foolishly mentioned earlier. Her first reaction was out-and-out refusal. However, when he countered with a pointed suggestion that he bungle his way there alone, calling Mike Riordon at his office for directions if he happened to get lost, she gritted her teeth and led the way to the nearest subway station.

As they rushed along with the blur of people making their way down the ramp, he tugged at her arm. "Why are we running?"

"Because everyone else is running. Would you rather get knocked down and stomped on?"

"Okay. Why are *they* all running? I mean, it's three in the afternoon; it's not like they're late for work."

"They're running because this is Washington."

"Is that supposed to make sense?"

Ignoring him, she jogged on. When he stopped to read the sign at the fare machine, the collective impatience of the crowd behind them was nearly palpable. Cutting in front of him, Laurel jammed enough coins into the slot for two fares and thrust a ticket his way.

"Hang on to it," she ordered over her shoulder as she ran for a quickly filling car. "You'll need it to get off."

"I'm not so sure I even want to get on," Sawyer muttered as the doors whooshed shut just behind him. "Is it always like this?"

"Yep. Welcome to the big city, Tex," she drawled in an impressive resurrection of her old accent.

They were both hanging on to ceiling straps for balance. Even so, when the train started moving, Laurel swayed against him. Sawyer responded by winding one arm around her hips, anchoring her to his side. For an embarrassingly brief moment, she thought of protesting, then decided not to bother. After all, it was only a few stops until they would be getting off. And besides, despite an occasional, flirtatious suggestion to the contrary, Sawyer had made it very clear how he really felt about her. During that awful moment back at the park, his eyes, his tone, his expression, had all proclaimed in the iciest of terms that whatever tender feelings he'd once had for her were dead. Obviously, this unfinished business he kept carping about was no more than some form of emotional revenge on her for her leaving him.

Deep down, Laurel knew that when she finally had time to sit down alone and digest that fact, she was going to come apart in a very dangerous way. That's why she was resolutely pushing it aside, filing it way back in her mind somewhere while she struggled to make it through this emotional roller coaster of a day. Keep it light and you'll make it, she reminded herself, trying and failing to ignore the anything-but-light sensations sizzling through her as his body rocked and rubbed against hers, perhaps a bit more frequently than strictly necessitated by the smooth motion of the train.

"Somehow," Sawyer said, bringing his mouth close to her ear to be heard over the noise, "I never imagined Washington to be this . . . frantic. I would have thought it a very sedate sort of city."

"Oh, it has its sedate side," Laurel assured him. "But a city predominantly populated by type-A personalities is not going to chug along at a snail's pace."

"Is that their problem?" he asked in a whisper, giving a conspiratorial nod at all the people wearing Rolex watches and carrying designer briefcases.

"I'm afraid so," she replied, chuckling. "Super-achievers. They can't bear to stand still. That's why they run everywhere."

He nodded with feigned solemnity. "Eager to get ahead."

"Or else eager to get a seat so they can read the latest journal of the Woodrow Wilson Center for Scholars."

He followed her gaze to the intense-looking young woman sitting close by, a "Lawyers Against Apartheid" button prominently pinned to her lapel. In her lap was a tome with that very title.

Their smothered laughter blended, unnoticed by anyone but the two of them. With a glance, Sawyer drew her attention to a bespectacled man a few seats away who was feverishly scribbling in an open notebook in his lap.

"If I'd known a Filofax was de rigueur for subway riding here, I'd have brought mine along."

Laurel nodded with exaggerated understanding. "I feel positively naked riding without one."

His eyes suddenly gleamed with dark lights she might have easily misread as serious interest if she hadn't known better.

"What an intriguing thought," he murmured.

"I was speaking figuratively, of course."

"What a coincidence. *Figuratively* is exactly how I was thinking." His eyes made a long, hot sweep of her body. "And what I think is that I'm more impressed now than I was eleven years ago."

Laurel tried to fight the insane burst of pleasure his words elicited. "You're also more of a flirt than you were eleven years ago. Although I can't for the life of me figure out why you're wasting your efforts on me."

"Can't you?" He made no effort to curb a cynical chuckle. "I shouldn't think it would be all that tough to figure out. I've already told you that we—"

"Have unfinished business," she interjected on a heavy note of disgust. "Whatever the hell that means."

"Curious?"

"Yes," she spat out irritably. "Satisfied?"

"Far from it. Although I plan to be before I'm done with you." There was a disturbingly confident quality to his smirk. "For now, though, it's enough to know that I've succeeded in stimulating your curiosity."

"The way I've stimulated yours?"

"Among other things. Are you ever going to open up and tell me about the past eleven years?"

Laurel shrugged, gazing out the window behind him. "You haven't asked . . . specifically."

"Why bother? Every time you come close to talking about yourself, your eyes glaze over and your jaw turns into a steel trap. Hell, you wouldn't even answer questions about your job when I asked. Not that I'm trying to put any pressure on you," he added magnanimously, shifting position so she was no longer able to look past him. "After all, we have all week . . . that's enough time for a man who's waited as long as I have."

He was back on that again. You'd think he'd spent those years in a monastery, which she had no doubt was far from the case. At any rate Laurel was getting sick of hearing about his long-suffering wait. Before she could tell him so, the train rolled to a stop at M Street. Brushing his arm away, she stalked out the door and joined the stampede up the ramp. When she reached the sidewalk, he was right at her heels, but fortunately she'd cooled down enough to realize that the safest thing to do was to abandon their volatile conversation topic.

"The National Geographic Society is this way," she told him, turning onto 17th Street. "I think you'll really be impressed by this globe. It's eleven feet in diameter, the largest in the world supposedly. I read somewhere that . . ."

She kept up the tour guide spiel all the way there, denying him any graceful opportunity to steer the conversation in a more personal direction. An occasional surreptitious glance at Sawyer revealed that he was nodding along, his lips curled in an amused smile that said he knew exactly what she was doing, and would go along with it. For now.

His attitude kept Laurel feeling the way she had for most of the day, slightly off-balance, torn between wanting to run and wanting to throw caution to the wind and unload years' worth of secrets and worries onto his broad shoulders. Sawyer was more than the first—the only—man she'd ever loved. He was the best friend she'd ever had as well. That fact was an insidious threat to all her carefully erected defenses.

The globe that Sawyer wanted to see was located on the first floor, the centerpiece of Explorer's Hall. Suspended over a reflecting pool and illuminated with special lights, it was a breathtaking sight. Even *he* was impressed into silence when he first glimpsed it. Together they slowly moved along the polished wooden rail that encircled the exhibit. It was nearly closing time and they were alone in the hall. The sheer magnitude of the sight before them and the museumlike hush invoked a special feeling of closeness.

"I'm glad we came," Sawyer said finally, his voice the sort of deep whisper that seemed proper for the moment.

"Me, too," Laurel responded just as softly. "I had forgotten how beautiful this is." She paused, then impulsively added, "I know it sounds crazy, but it always gives me goose bumps."

He just nodded, and for once his smile conveyed understanding rather than amusement. Maybe it was that —that reassuring smile from her past—or maybe it was just the mood of security created by the dim lights and silence that lifted Laurel's spirit to the top of the wall she'd built around herself. With the world suspended before her, a slow-moving river of memories flowed through her mind, without her control or censor. Idly, her gaze drifted over the globe, tracing the path of her life.

"When I first arrived in Washington," she said, her voice sounding safely small and inconsequential in the huge hall, "I used to come here—sometimes on my lunch hour, always at least once on the weekend—and just stare at it. It made me feel . . . I don't know, safer, more in control maybe, to see the place where I'd come from and the place where I was now. I liked seeing for myself that they were close and yet far enough apart that they didn't overlap. And I guess I liked seeing how far I'd come."

With his index finger, Sawyer traced a path in the air. "All the way from Beaumont to Washington, D.C. Quite an accomplishment really. I know I haven't said it yet—actually I've been pretty rough on you—but the truth is I'm damn proud of you, Laurel."

The name had come almost automatically that time, but to Sawyer it still felt strange on his tongue. Hell, she was still Dory. Especially at moments like this, with the guarded expression gone from her face and her eyes that soft, dreamy shade of green he'd never seen anywhere else, she seemed to be his Dory. Even though, deep down, he knew that wasn't so. She was someone else now and in no way his. She was an enigma, part stranger, part memory. Familiar and yet a mystery. He had to come to terms with the fact that he no longer knew this woman beside him, if indeed he ever had.

"Proud of me?" She tipped her head back to look up at him in disbelief. "That's not what I would have guessed you were feeling. Angry, disappointed, maybe, but proud?" She shook her head.

"Angry, disappointed, *and* proud."

It took a few seconds for Sawyer to figure out what it was that made her short laugh sound odd. It was the bitterness in it. Bitterness shadowed her face as well, and he knew—without knowing how—that it was 100 percent self-directed.

"Well, you wouldn't be," she said emphatically, "if you knew the truth."

"Laurel," he said, wanting to know what the hell she was so tense about, but wanting even more to soothe her, "nothing, absolutely nothing you could tell me would lessen my opinion of you or my respect for all you've achieved."

Again she gave that short, grating laugh and the look in her eyes turned a little wild.

"Oh, no? Well, try this . . . it's a lie, Sawyer." She hardly moved except for the slight heave of her shoulders, but suddenly she seemed to crumble right before his eyes. "Oh, God help me, it's all a lie."

Chapter Four

"WHAT'S A LIE, baby?" Without thinking, Sawyer had gathered her into his arms. Above the concern for her that overrode most other thought pounded a rush of satisfaction that she wasn't tightening up and pulling away. Instead, she seemed quite content to rest her head against his chest. "Tell me what's the matter, sweetheart."

"*I'm* what's the matter."

She stopped to choke in a deep breath, and he knew she was fighting back tears. A good crying jag might be the best thing for her. She reminded him of a tightly capped bottle of seltzer that had been shaken too hard. That was one reason he hadn't pressed her more today, even though he was burning to know everything that had happened to her during the years they'd been apart. At the time he hadn't realized exactly why he'd held back, but now he knew. On some level he'd been aware that she wasn't simply reluctant to talk about her past, or being coy about it. She was scared to death.

"Let it go," he murmured against the sweet-scented silkiness of her hair. "You're with me now, sweetheart. Sawyer. You can tell me anything. You always could."

"Not this," she said in a tight voice.

"Shhh. Anything. What did you mean, it's all a lie?"

There was a silence, then a long, shuddering sigh against his slightly damp shirt front before she answered.

"Me. I'm the lie. Laurel Forrest. I'm not who anyone thinks I am."

"You're talking about your name," he said, holding back a relieved chuckle.

So Laurel Forrest was still saddled with Dory Milinkus's scrupulous sense of honor. All these years she'd probably been fighting with her conscience over using a phony name, and seeing him again had tipped the scales against her. "Darlin', lots of people change their names. It's nothing to lose sleep over. You can even make it legal if it makes you feel better, you know."

"It is legal," Laurel told him, lifting her head and meeting his eyes with a tortured expression. "And it's not what I'm talking about."

"What are you talking about?" His tone was intentionally easy, masking, he hoped, his surge of concern for her.

"It's very complicated . . . no, that's another lie. Really it's not all that complicated; it's just very hard for me to talk about."

He stroked her hair, soothing. "Take your time."

They both looked up abruptly as the sound of briskly approaching footsteps intruded on their privacy. An elderly guard appeared, stopping to unlock a panel of wall switches.

"I hate to throw you good folks out," he said with a

friendly grin, "but I'm afraid that's exactly what I have to do." He tapped his watch. "Closing time. Come back tomorrow, why don't you?"

"Maybe we'll do that," Sawyer replied distractedly, his anxious attention focusing on Laurel. Great. Just when she'd been close to opening up to him. Well, he'd be damned if he'd let her freeze up again just because of bad timing.

"Let's go," he said, grabbing her hand and leading her outside.

Evidently, it was closing time for many shops and offices throughout the city as well. The sidewalks were already overtaken by a steady stream of humanity moving in both directions. He pulled Laurel along for several minutes, vainly searching for a quiet place to sit, and maybe have a cup of coffee, before she tugged him to a halt beside a recessed doorway. By standing on the top step, they managed to stay out of the path of everyone else.

"Do you have any idea where you're going?" she asked.

Sawyer thought about faking it so he wouldn't lose control of the situation, but her smile told him the question had been purely rhetorical. He shrugged. "No."

"I thought not. Your hotel is that way." She indicated the direction they'd just come from.

"Good. Because I'm not ready to go back to my hotel yet. Unless, of course, you're ready to come with me."

A frown puckered her brow. "Sawyer, I . . . I'm tired."

"So am I. Tired of us playing games with each other as if there was never anything more between us than a teenage crush."

"Maybe that's all there ever was." She sighed, and he would have been furious if her eyes, her tone, everything about her weren't screaming that she didn't for a minute believe that.

"Bullshit," he said.

She gave in to a small, reluctant smile. "That's putting it bluntly."

"You bet. Now are you going to help me find someplace quiet where we can talk or am I going to have to drag you halfway around this city looking?"

"I'll help, I'll help," she said, surrendering with a small laugh. After a few seconds of thought she looked up at him with another, even more reluctant smile. "The only place I know of that will be quiet at this time of day is my place."

That was better than Sawyer had hoped for. He'd thought it would take days for her to feel comfortable enough to bring him home. Trying hard not to look like a teenage boy invited into the cheerleader's dressing room, he smiled. "You know best."

"I have my doubts about that," she muttered. "But come on, the metro's this way."

Sawyer yanked her to a halt before she'd taken half a step, steering her to the curb. "Oh, no you don't," he said firmly. "Once was enough on that monster. This time we're doing it my way."

Lifting the arm that wasn't holding her to his side, he signaled for a taxi, reveling in the way Laurel's smug expression melted into astonishment when one pulled over almost immediately. Even with the rush-hour traffic, the drive to her College Park apartment on the city's north side was reasonably short. Despite his best efforts at small talk, however, Laurel was silent for most of the ride, and he knew she was trying to think of a way to tactfully get out of finishing the discussion they'd begun in the museum. There was no way he'd allow it, of course, but Sawyer figured he'd probably come across as a little too heavy-handed if he said so.

Instead, he limited himself to innocuous comments about the city landscaping, asking if the trees were always this well foliated so early in April and received an enthusiastic lecture on horticulture from their gregarious driver for his trouble. Laurel, meanwhile, continued to gaze out the window with a worried expression. She was still wearing it when they reached her apartment on the second floor of what looked to him like the quintessential Washington home. It was built entirely of brick, with shiny black shutters on the numerous small-paned windows and elaborately detailed molding surrounding a solid-looking front door.

Laurel's apartment itself took him by surprise. Ruefully, he realized that he'd foolishly been expecting something with signs of transience, as if the last eleven years had all been a misunderstanding. This, though, was a home. The home of a woman with very definite style and tastes.

"Very nice," he said as he closed the door and took a long interested look around.

It was annoyingly more than nice—large and airy, with dark-toned oriental carpets on the polished wood floors and lots of cream and almond tones everywhere else. To Sawyer, it all seemed to come together in a way he thought of as magazine-layout perfect. The colors and style were different, but it looked similar to the way his own house did when that high-priced Dallas decorator had finished. He wondered if Laurel had done this herself. Dory never could have, he was certain, and again he was reminded that he didn't have any idea of what sort of things Laurel Forrest was capable.

That brought him full circle back to her strange comment about herself being the lie, and he decided not to get sidetracked by asking if she'd done her own decorating. He wanted as few distractions as possible between them and the topic they'd come here to discuss.

"Would you like something to drink?" Laurel asked. She'd been moving through the apartment, opening windows. A mild breeze ruffled her honey-brown hair and made the lace curtains behind her dance. "A glass of wine, maybe?"

Looking at her standing there, framed by the late-afternoon sunlight, her white pleated slacks and blue silk blouse clinging gently to her soft curves, Sawyer suddenly felt like he could use something a good deal stronger than wine.

"Wine sounds good," he said.

He followed her to the door of the kitchen, a sleek, efficient, seldom-used-looking room, then ambled back through the living room, trying to catch up on eleven years' worth of her interests by glancing at book titles and album covers. Anne Tyler and Z. Z. Top. No easy answers here. He considered following his strong urge to take a look at her bedroom, but decided against it. The sight of even one thing in there belonging to Jasper Dane would definitely render him unfit company for the rest of the evening.

His intense resentment—jealousy, really—of Dane was something he couldn't figure out. If he didn't want Dane having Laurel, it would seem to follow that he wanted her himself. And, of course, he didn't. He wouldn't have her back in his life in any real sort of way even if she begged him. Not that it wouldn't be soul satisfying to have her at least show a spark of interest in that direction. No, he was well over Dory, and the only interest he had in Laurel Forrest was as a friend. And, of course, eventually, before this week was over, collecting on a very old debt.

"Here you go." Laurel returned carrying two glasses of wine.

Accepting the one she handed to him, Sawyer took a long sip and held it for a moment, staring into the distance with a thoughtful expression. "Ah, it's extremely. . ." he hesitated, relishing Laurel's expression of amazement as she waited for his reaction. "Wet," he finally pronounced. "And white . . . with unmistakable signs of staying that way."

She rolled her eyes. "For a minute there I thought you'd picked up some culture. But I guess some things never change."

"Almost everything changes, Laurel," he said, quickly shedding the joking mood he'd used to soothe her nervousness. "Everything and everybody. But sometimes parts of things stay the same. The part of me that was your friend is still there."

Laurel sipped her wine self-consciously. And what about the part of you that was my love? she felt a strong need to ask. Only an even stronger fear of the answer, whatever it might be, held her back.

"I think I could use a friend about now," she marshaled the courage to admit.

"You've got one, sweetheart." Pulling her along, he moved to the sofa and sat down in the middle, leaving only enough room for her to squeeze in between his hitched-up leg and the arm. "This is probably the most tactless, boorish way I could possibly handle this, but I'm afraid that's what comes naturally . . . What is this lie that's got you so tied up in knots?"

Her shoulders lifted in a shrug that drove home to him just how small and fragile she was, and Sawyer longed to pull her against him again. Instead, he stretched his arm along the back of the sofa so that they were just touching, the wispy strands of her hair like electric wires against his skin, and waited.

"I'm not really sure how to begin. Believe me," she said with an awkward laugh, "I've never told anyone about this before."

"I'm honored," he said truthfully. Somehow, when she appeared vulnerable this way, it was easier for him to admit that he still cared. Not the way he once did, naturally, but he still didn't like seeing her upset or, worse, in trouble. He would do what he could to help. Just as he would for any old friend, he told himself.

"I guess I should start at the beginning," she said.

"Not a bad idea."

"Do you remember what you said about your success starting with an accident?"

Sawyer nodded.

"Well, so did mine. Only, it wasn't an accident in my case, it was a lie."

"I think you better slow down."

Laurel paused to gather her thoughts, mentally filtering hundreds of little details Sawyer had no way of knowing, quickly deciding which were important and discarding the rest.

"When I left Beaumont," she began, "I had no idea where I was heading. I was hurt and angry and desperate. You and I had always talked about seeing New York, so that's where I went first." She looked at him with a sheepish expression. "But it wasn't at all the way I dreamed it would be. It was hot and noisy and... overwhelming. I couldn't even find a room I wasn't afraid to stay in where one night wouldn't cost most of what I'd saved. So I finally got back on a bus and headed for the airport. Then I bought a ticket for the furthest place away that I could afford. London."

"London?" He was stunned to learn just how far from him she had felt she needed to run. It was ridiculous, he knew, but all the old pain and bitterness, along with that stinking feeling of helplessness, was roiling up inside him. "Let me get this straight. New York scared the hell out of you, so you decided to try another big city half a world away?"

"I was setting a trap for myself," she explained. "I knew if I didn't do something drastic, I would go crawling home in no time."

"Back to me, you mean?"

"You had nothing to do with it."

"Thanks."

"I didn't mean it that way. Can't you even try to understand why I left? I wasn't running from you, Sawyer... I was running *for* me."

It was a painful effort to unclench his jaw, but Sawyer managed. "I guess I can understand. I still don't agree, though," he added quickly.

Laurel decided it was a losing battle to try and explain yet again. "Anyway, I knew that without enough money to go home I'd be forced to make it on my own ... to find a place to live and a job."

"And did you?"

"Yes. It was on the plane on the way over that I came up with my new name. Cut it out," she ordered when he winced at the mere mention of it. "I combined the names of the two most elegant-looking brides in the *New York Times* society pages."

"Too bad you weren't reading the sports pages at the time, instead."

"Say whatever you want, I still think it sounds ... sophisticated," she finished triumphantly.

Lord, she was magnificent, thought Sawyer, squaring off against him with her chin up, her green eyes flashing defiantly. "Yeah, well, I guess it grows on you. So was Laurel Forrest a smash in London?"

"Not quite. I did manage to find a room I could afford in a small rooming house near University College. The landlady was a real motherly type who took a liking to me right away." Her eyes sparkled devilishly. "Of course, my story about being a poor orphan whose parents had died in a boating accident and whose dastardly older brother had squandered the family fortune helped my case immensely."

Sawyer squinted at her. "You didn't actually tell people that?"

"I did," she admitted, smiling sadly. "Wait. It gets worse. Mrs. Taylor—my landlady—bullied the professor who lived next door into helping me get a job at the university. I was only a file clerk in the registrar's office, but I felt like somebody for the first time in my life. As an employee I could take courses at a reduced rate, so I was going to class every night. I made friends who knew nothing about my past or my family. I had a room I liked where I could invite them whenever I felt like it. Without," she added bitterly, "having to worry about my father ranting and raving or, worse, being passed out drunk on the floor."

"Sounds like paradise."

The undercurrents of resentment in his voice made Laurel feel miserable.

"Far from it," she snapped. "Do you want to hear that I was lonely? That I missed you? Well, I did. I made friends, yes, but I could never let any of them get too close or the truth about me might slip out. And the one person I wanted most, the one person I wanted to share everything with, didn't want to be with me."

"Can it . . . *Laurel*. That's crap and we both know it."

"You're unbelievable," she cried, trying to unwedge herself from the sofa. "I don't know why I ever thought I could talk to you about this in the first place."

Sawyer felt something close to panic and backed down hard on the urge to pin her in place. Settling for holding her in her seat with a minimum of force, he strove to sound contrite.

"All right, I'm sorry I questioned what you said. I think maybe both of our feelings on that particular subject are still a little . . . raw. Why don't we just steer clear of it, okay?"

Steer clear of it, Laurel thought, fighting an ironic laugh. How could they when it sat between them like Mount Rushmore?

"All right," she agreed. "I guess we can try."

"Good. So you got a job and took some classes. What then?"

"I worked there for three years and eventually was promoted from clerk to receptionist at the front desk. It seems silly now, but at the time that was a very big deal. By taking summer courses, I also managed to earn three years' worth of credits, even though I was officially considered a part-time student." Her mouth suddenly twisted in a wry smile. "Then a new girl was hired for the office—Lady something-or-other—and she didn't fancy being stuck in a back room handling dusty old files. It seems her father thought gainful employment was just what she needed to curb a wild streak, so in order to make her happy, he pulled some strings and *voilà!* She's at the front desk and I'm back slinging files."

"That's rough," Sawyer said with a sympathetic shake of his head.

"Correction: That's life. It's who you know, not what you know and all that. Suddenly, all my hard work meant nothing, and I had this sinking feeling that it was always going to be that way. I looked around at my new life, which had seemed so good up until then, and realized I was still a long way from the success and glamour and excitement that I'd sacrificed so much in search of."

That I'd sacrificed you for, she wanted to say, to somehow make him understand that even then, three years after she'd left him, she had still felt the loss as if it were a physical pain. It wasn't being demoted, but the realization that she'd given up everything she'd ever loved for nothing that drove her to such a point of desperation. However, she couldn't think of words that would come close to convincing Sawyer of that, which would penetrate that cold wall of remoteness he built up whenever the subject arose.

"So don't tell me," he was saying, calmly oblivious to her suffering, "you quit."

"Not right away. First, I sulked and simmered about it for a few weeks, then I came up with an absolutely brilliant idea. I could avenge myself on the powers that be who decided social position should be rewarded before initiative and loyalty, and at the same time take a giant step toward getting everything I wanted out of life. I was scared to death, of course—but I kept remembering that I'd also been scared when I first stepped off that plane at Heathrow and became Laurel Forrest, and that had worked out fine in the end. So I did it."

"For God's sake, Laurel, did what?"

"Oh, I'm sorry," she said with an uneasy laugh. "I lied about my college records."

After all that, it sounded so anticlimactic. Sawyer stared at her, his eyes narrowed in confusion, as if there had to be something more, something suitably horrendous to justify the dramatic buildup she'd given the announcement.

"Actually, I did more than lie about it," she explained hastily in an effort to make him understand how significant her sin truly was. "One night when I was working late alone, I pulled my own transcript and filled in all the courses and grades I needed to graduate. With honors," she added. "Then I replaced it with the transcripts of those already graduated. *Then* I quit."

Clamping her mouth shut, she waited for his reaction. Lord, she never thought she'd have to strain to convince anyone of the seriousness of what she'd done. It was probably even some sort of authentic crime, for pity's sake. Didn't he realize that? Then again, maybe that's why he was looking at her in that strange, undecided way. He couldn't think of anything despicable enough to express his feelings.

"That," he finally proclaimed, "is the most incredible thing I've ever heard."

Sawyer had a wild urge to throw back his head and roar, but he couldn't tell from Laurel's expression how she would interpret that. She might mistakenly think he was laughing at her. Or worse, that he wasn't taking her problem seriously. He was beginning to get an idea of why she was so uptight about this. It meant her whole life was built on quicksand. Christ, did Dane know anything about it? Somehow he strongly doubted it, and that made him feel pleased as hell.

For sure, it was going to be one complicated mess to straighten out, but for now he couldn't get past this crazy feeling of gut-level pride. It had been such a . . . a ballsy thing to do. He could just picture her working on those records, her brow tight, her green eyes aflame with an expression of fierce righteousness. Of course, he knew her well enough to know that later she would have suffered from extreme pangs of guilt. In fact, he was surprised she hadn't broken back into the place to undo it all.

"So the truth is," he began, carefully keeping his voice neutral, "that you never actually completed college?"

"Well, in a way I did. I mean, since then I've taken all the courses I needed, here and there, and—" She broke off with a sigh. "Actually, technically, no, I've never graduated."

"Then how did you end up as special assistant in the Office of Protocol, for God's sake?"

"Under false pretenses, obviously," she admitted, twisting a clump of hair around her finger like a ribbon of brown satin. It was a nervous habit, and, watching, Sawyer suddenly felt twenty years old again. "So you can see what an . . . awkward position I'm in. After I quit the college, I rummaged up enough courage to apply for an office job at the American embassy, and by some quirk of fate I got it."

"Without any kind of security check?" demanded Sawyer in amazement.

"Oh, they ran a security check," she replied, "background, lie-detector tests, the works. I don't know how or why—because I was so nervous I lost six pounds in three days—but it all worked out. Of course, I told them the truth about my name and I didn't tell them that story about my parents being killed. That was when I discovered that if you have to lie, the best thing to do is keep it as close to the truth as possible."

"Like admitting you come from Beaumont, but changing neighborhoods?"

"Right," she acknowledged with a sheepish nod. "It's all so intertwined now that sometimes *I* even get confused about what's real and what isn't. Like my name. My boss at the embassy finally helped me to have it changed legally, and now it feels right, like I've always been Laurel Forrest. It's Pandora Milinkus that sounds unreal."

There was a sudden, sharp pain in Sawyer's gut. One he knew he was a jerk for feeling. So, with one simple remark she'd just negated her entire life before leaving Beaumont, a life he'd *thought* he'd been an important part of. Had he really expected anything else?

"What do you plan to do about this little . . . ah, problem?" he asked.

"I wish I knew. At first I was so thrilled to have the job I didn't think of the risks involved. But as I gradually began working my way up, I became more and more worried that somehow someone would discover what I'd done. That's why I transferred to Washington. I'd hoped some distance might help."

"Did it?"

"Not a bit." Weariness etched her face. "Sometimes I feel my whole life is like a house of cards built by the edge of the ocean. I'm just waiting for the tide to come in and send it all crashing."

"It seems to me," ventured Sawyer, "that you've got two choices. You can come clean and take your chances . . . after all, you've made an effort to rectify the situation by taking those courses for which you forged grades."

"After the fact."

He shrugged. "As I said, you take your chances that your boss will understand that. Or you just keep on going. I'd say that at this point the odds are with you keeping it secret."

Laurel tried to feel reassured by that, but it was impossible. Would he still think the odds were with her if he knew that in the very near future she might be returning to the scene of the crime? *Wife of U.S. Ambassador a Fraud.* At night the endless possibilities for colorful headlines ran like tickertape through her nightmares.

"Anyway, what's the absolute worst that can happen?" Sawyer's tone was casual, as if they were discussing the spread on a pro football game instead of her whole life.

"Oh, not much. I could just lose everything, that's what can happen," she countered irritably. "My job, all my friends who probably wouldn't be so friendly if they discovered I'd been lying to them for years, the future I've worked and planned and sacrificed for. That's all. For all intents and purposes, Laurel Forrest would cease to exist."

"You'd still have Dory Milinkus."

Laurel shuddered. "God forbid."

"Would it really be that bad?"

"It would be a disaster, a nightmare. For me it would be like starting over again at less than zero."

Sawyer was torn between irritation with her for being such a damn snob and a wild urge to defend Dory . . . and himself. How could he have possibly thought this woman needed him? Obviously, all she needed was a place on the next rung up the ladder to plant her designer shoe.

Oh, he was going to relish paying her back. He'd thought long and hard through the years about what form his revenge would take. And now he knew. He had no interest in exposing her or ruining her self-satisfied life. He no longer even had a desire to rub her nose in his own success, to flaunt the fact that he drove a Jaguar, owned the biggest house in town overlooking the ocean, had bought the country club he once had no hope of even joining. No, there was only one thing he wanted—needed—to ease the frustration that had been building inside him for eleven years. That was to possess Laurel or Dory or whoever the hell she really was in the most fundamental way a man can possess a woman.

"You're a smart lady, Laurel." His voice had become a smooth soft drawl that tripped an alarm in Laurel's head. "There's no denying that. But you have this annoying blind spot when it comes to your past."

"I don't have any blind spot." Although he hadn't moved an inch, she suddenly felt like he was closing in on her. Without thinking, she retreated back against the well-padded arm of the sofa.

"Yes, you do. You're blind to anything in your past that was good or right. For instance." Now he definitely *was* moving closer, his head slowly lowering until their eyes were level, his mouth so close that his breath heated her cheek. "There was a lot that Dory Milinkus found good and pleasurable in life."

"I never said there wasn't." Her own voice was a shaky, uncertain whisper, and Laurel vaguely thought how that wouldn't do at all. She should be acting crisp and in control if she wanted to halt the wayward turn their conversation had taken. But it was difficult to stay in control with his taut body so close, providing a barrier between her and the rest of the world.

"True, you never said there wasn't," Sawyer allowed, "but you also never said there was. The truth is, you never talk about the good times, never give any indication that you even remember them."

"So?"

"So, I think it's time I refreshed your memory for you."

"And how do you plan to do that?"

What was wrong with her? Asking such a question, a leading question, of a man who obviously was ready and willing to be led.

"Like this."

Her belated protest was choked off by his lips, warm and damp and tasting slightly of wine. Desire exploded inside Laurel. He'd caught her with her defenses down, tired from the long day and fresh from having bared her soul to him. Drinking wine on an empty stomach hadn't helped to keep her levelheaded, either. His mouth, moving over hers with gentle expertise, seemed the perfect balm for all that was wrong with her life.

Just as it had last night on the terrace, the familiarity of his scent and touch and the way his body felt hard and lean against hers was triggering long-dormant responses in Laurel. Her arms lifted to circle his neck, pulling him closer as her fingers curled in the thick waves of his hair. With a deep groan, Sawyer tugged her lower on the sofa, then slowly pressed his body against hers at the same instant his tongue surged between her teeth.

He kissed her lazily, carefully, exploring all the sleek and rough textures of her mouth. Then, suddenly, the long unhurried strokes of his tongue and the waves of pleasure they sent breaking over her stopped, and Laurel opened her eyes to find him watching her. His eyes were midnight blue and lit with an unholy amusement.

"You were much better at this when you were eighteen," he accused. "Then you used to kiss me back. Try it."

His mouth returned to hers and Laurel obediently slid her lips lightly across his.

"With your tongue, Laurel," he ordered, prodding her with his own for emphasis.

Defiantly, Laurel clamped her hand onto the back of his head and kissed him deeply, with enough enthusiasm to send his temperature soaring. She suddenly remembered how he used to like to feel her hands on his chest and on impulse she did that, too, sliding them under his blue cotton shirt and swirling a path of gentle caresses higher until her fingers slid over the flat buds of his nipples. Sawyer's shoulders jerked. Drawing in a harsh, ragged breath, he lifted his head to look down at her. The lazy look of passion that had glowed in his eyes just a moment ago had evolved into one of intense masculine hunger.

"No one," he declared in a soft rasp of a voice, "no one ever wanted anyone as much as I want you right now."

It was flattering and a bit frightening to be the object of such untempered desire. For Laurel, the flattered euphoria of the moment lasted until Sawyer's fingers moved to her top blouse button and flicked it open. The second followed quickly, exposing the lace edge of her bra. Panicking, she grabbed his hand and held it pressed between her breasts.

This, too, was familiar—the sensual pleasure of having Sawyer peel off her blouse and bra and the uninhibited exploration of her body that was sure to follow. Unfortunately, she also remembered what came after that, the arguing and the moodiness when she inevitably called a halt. She had a feeling that Sawyer would handle frustration even less graciously now than he had years ago.

"No," she said as his eyes, dark and passion glazed, flashed impatiently. "We have to stop."

"Give me one good reason why."

"Because we—" She broke off abruptly.

His eyes had narrowed and his mouth was tipped up at the corners in cynical amusement. He was ready for her all right, ready to laugh at all her old reasons for refusing to make love with him.

"Why should we stop, Laurel? You can't hand me that old line about being afraid of getting pregnant and being stuck in Beaumont for the rest of your life." His hand moved beneath hers, his thumb stroking the side of her breast. "Do you ever wonder what your life would be like now if you *had* stayed with me? If you'd had my babies?"

The thought of it brought Laurel a sudden, sharp yearning. "Yes," she whispered. "I've thought about it."

"You wouldn't be running scared the way you are now, that's for sure. Or worrying that your life might blow up in your face any second. Of course," he murmured with that same taunting half smile, "you also wouldn't be Laurel Forrest."

Laurel's eyelids fluttered shut in confusion. She felt as if she was walking a tightrope stretched between two different lives. No, worse, between two conflicting halves of herself. And on both sides there were temptations and fears. Eventually, she would have to let herself fall one way or the other, but at the moment she wasn't sure which way she wanted to go. Opening her eyes, she drew a deep breath, prepared to offer Sawyer the one reason he might respect, one that would buy her the time she needed to decide who she wanted to be.

"We have to stop because . . . because I'm going to marry Jasper Dane," she finished in a rush, before she could change her mind.

For a few seconds, shock and an agonizing look of pain burned in Sawyer's eyes, and she wished she could take the words back. Then the shutters drew closed, locking whatever he was feeling out of sight.

"When?" he demanded.

"I . . . I . . ." Laurel's voice fumbled under his black stare. "We haven't exactly set the date . . . it's still sort of unofficial."

His lips kicked up in an insolent smile. "In that case, congratulations. Let me be the first to kiss the bride."

He did, savagely, and with an insulting thoroughness that brought tears to Laurel's eyes and left her lips stinging.

"Stop it," she cried, shoving at his shoulders. "You don't understand. I really am going to marry him ... I'm not playing some sort of game."

"Neither am I," he countered harshly. "And I do understand. Perfectly. Now I think you should understand something. You can marry the entire House of Representatives for all I care, and it won't change one important fact. You owe me, lady."

Chapter Five

"OWE YOU?" LAUREL echoed, not nearly as in the dark about his meaning as she tried to appear. "I don't know what you're talking about."

"I'm talking about all those times you asked me to stop, to wait, when I wanted you so much I thought I'd die from it. Well, I waited... eleven years. And now I'm here to collect."

"That's crazy."

"Not to me."

"Relationships end, Sawyer. You can't waltz back into someone's life years later and try to collect on an old promise."

"I can. And I am."

His voice was hard, but his hands, sliding over her shoulders and arms, were gentle—and strangely soothing considering the nature of their position and conversation and the glint of grim determination in his eyes. Amazingly, she was not the least bit afraid.

"Besides, he continued in a gruff voice, "it never felt like what we had came to an end. More like it was . . . interrupted. Do you know what it's like to go on year after year feeling in some weird sort of way as if part of your life is on hold?"

Laurel closed her eyes to the sudden anger in his. "I think so," she admitted softly.

After a moment he asked quietly, "And do you ever wonder what it would have been like for us if we had made love?"

She'd wondered all right. Memories of countless nights alone in her bed when frustration and fantasies kept sleep at bay flashed before her.

"Tell me, Laurel," he ordered, giving her shoulders a rough shake. "Tell me you've thought about it just like I have."

"I've . . . I've thought about it," she confessed.

"Now open your eyes and tell me you don't want this to happen almost as much as I do."

Laurel obeyed, opening her eyes and without speaking a word telling him much more than she knew was wise.

"Give me one good reason not to make love to you," he challenged for the second time that evening. Only this time his voice was as silky and caressing as the hypnotic movement of his hands on her body.

"Jasper . . ." she ventured, trying to fight a powerful insurrection of her senses.

Sawyer shook his head. "That's not a good reason. You don't love him, Laurel. If you did, you would have told him all the things you just confided in me instead. And you sure as hell wouldn't be lying under me with your body so soft and hot that it feels like it's melting."

He knew that as surely as he knew the sun would rise in the morning. And he thanked God for the underlying sense of honor that was as much a part of her as that smile that had the power to light up his world. "Try again, darlin'."

"We can't just pick up where we left off, Sawyer. Things have changed, we've changed."

"Uh-uh. Nothing's changed. Not really. If it had, you wouldn't have felt you could tell me things that you've never told another living soul. You wouldn't have trusted me with secrets that could destroy you."

Even as Sawyer said the words, the earth-shattering truth of them exploded inside his head. She might not like the idea, but the fact was that she trusted him with her life. That realization brought a rush of pleasure so strong he trembled. He was probably a fool, but he couldn't help the glimmer of hope that sprouted deep inside him.

"Why couldn't you have trusted me that much eleven years ago?"

There was no bitterness in his voice this time, and no accusation. Just wistfulness and a deep note of regret that was echoed in every fiber of Laurel's body.

"I guess because I had to learn to have faith in myself before I could have that kind of faith in someone else."

"Trust me now, Laurel," he urged, pulling her closer. "Come to bed with me."

Laurel was swept by a calming sense of inevitability. She longed to melt against him, to simply close her eyes and her mind and be swept away in a blaze of passion that left no need for words. But in a way he'd been right—she did owe him something. She owed him more than a lukewarm surrender that at some later, more prudent moment, she could disavow as temporary insanity.

"Yes, Sawyer, please," she said, her voice quiet but rich with certitude. "Take me to bed and show me how it should have been."

Without a pause, he rolled to his feet and lifted her easily, cradling her against his rumpled shirt.

"I meant literally to bed," he informed her with a

smile. "I once made you a promise that the first time we made love we would have plenty of time and plenty of room. And a sofa is just too reminiscent of the back seat of a car."

His stride long and purposeful, he made his way to the bedroom and carefully lowered Laurel to her feet by the side of the queen-sized bed. With a quick sweep of his arm, the bright-flowered comforter and blanket beneath were peeled back, and gently he drew her down with him onto the cool, dark-blue sheets. Outside, the sun was beginning to set, spinning an amber glow that filtered through the lace curtains, illuminating the room as softly as candlelight.

Slowly, his cupped hands lifted to her face, touching her as if she were as fragile as blown glass. Just as slowly his mouth dipped to hers in a meeting that was more of a caress than a kiss. His lips were warm and gentle, moving over hers with the scantest pressure. Gradually, his tongue came into play, sliding lightly between her lips, lingering maddeningly at the corners until the mild yearning sensation in Laurel's belly became a fierce demand for more.

Threading her fingers through the silky thickness of his hair, she met his tongue with the tip of her own. It was like touching a match to a rain-starved forest. A groan that started deep in his chest raked over her, urging her on, and she boldly deepened the kiss. Her tongue thrust past his teeth, seeking the moist warmth beyond. She was breathless, tingling from her head to her toes, and very, very warm when Sawyer gently pulled away.

"It looks as if we might not need as much time as I thought," he observed, a telling note of huskiness in his soft chuckle.

The hands that had been holding her head dropped to her shoulders, then on to her half-buttoned blouse. Swiftly he removed it and reached around to unclasp her bra, tossing both aside. When she was naked from the waist up, he slowly lowered his gaze. Laurel could actually see his eyes darken with appreciation. Her nipples immediately puckered in response to the unspoken praise, drawing a gravelly laugh of delight from Sawyer.

"Do you know what it does to me to see you respond this way?" he murmured, reaching out to cup her breasts in his hands. They seemed to swell at his touch. "It makes me feel like conquering the world. And it makes me very, very impatient."

His hands moved aside and his mouth replaced them, opening to suck gently at each taut peak in turn. Her palms planted on the mattress for support, Laurel arched with pleasure, releasing a soft gasp of anticipation when she felt his fingers drop to the front of her slacks. The sounds of the snap and zipper being freed were lost in the quickening rush of their breathing. Then the slacks were sliding off her, her silk panties with them, and there was nothing between her and the warm, wanting look in Sawyer's eyes as he leaned back to stare at her.

It was the first time he had ever seen her completely naked, and he was unprepared for the hot rush of desire that poured through his body at the sight. He was also unprepared for the questioning look of vulnerability in her eyes.

"You're beautiful," he whispered. "More beautiful than ever."

Laurel shook her head, but before she could utter a syllable, he gathered her in his arms and told her with his hands and mouth that she was indeed more beautiful to him now than she had ever been—more beautiful than any woman he'd known before or since.

He whispered in her ear, against the sensitive skin of her throat, and with his open mouth pressed wetly to the full curve of her breast. He whispered lavish words of praise and blunt declarations of desire, telling her things that Laurel thought should probably make her blush, but that made her burn instead. His words and his touch chased away all possibility of coherent thought and Laurel was glad.

At the moment she didn't want to think coherently. She didn't want to think at all. She wanted to feel all the pleasures and sensations she'd foolishly denied herself before now. She wanted to forget about tomorrow and about making decisions and making choices and heed the clear, timeless call of her senses. And amazingly, more than anything she'd ever wanted before, she wanted to give herself completely to Sawyer Gates.

When he carefully disentangled himself from her embrace and stood, Laurel sounded a whimper of protest that quickly faded at the sight of him yanking at the buttons of his shirt, ripping one off in his haste. Her gaze washed over him, measuring the accuracy of her imagination against the mesmerizing reality of him. Reality was better. The arrow of dark hair covering his chest was wider and thicker than it had been eleven years ago. His shoulders were broader and the muscles in his deeply tanned arms more well defined, swelling above his elbows with an iron strength she had felt in his embrace. From elbow to wrist, they ran in taut cords that flexed as he reached for his belt buckle.

It was loosened with a metallic click, followed by the whoosh of his zipper and the rough slide of denim over flesh. His jeans and underwear came off together, banished to the bed post behind her with a negligent toss. Laurel sucked in her breath, wide-eyed at her first unfettered glimpse of his body. During those passionate, long-ago sessions in the back of Sawyer's car, she had explored him almost as eagerly and as fully as he did her. But never had she seen him like this, his body long and lean, backlit by the setting sun. He stood with his arms hanging loose by his sides, his stance characteristically self-assured, his need for her bold and unmistakable. A primitive part of Laurel, a part very close to her core, thrilled to the unabashed sight of it. With an impatient sound of desire, she opened her arms and he came to her.

It was Laurel's turn to relearn old secrets. Rolling to her side, she leisurely traced the intriguing curve of his biceps, loving the smooth resiliency of his flesh beneath her fingertips. She ruffled the hair on his chest, stroking his washboard ribs and hard, flat belly.

"You're skinny," she murmured, the words one more caress.

"Mmmm." He leaned to nibble her shoulder, then tickled the vulnerable spot behind her ear with his tongue. "Ah, you still like that."

"Yes, but I was supposed to be discovering what *you* like," Laurel pointed out with a giggle that disappeared as he used his teeth in an incredibly erotic caress of her throat. In a rush of desire her hand found and captured the hard, hot length of his arousal.

"I think you just did," he groaned, throwing his head back, his eyes tightly closed. "Ah, love, that feels good." A moment later, he opened his eyes and smiled at her ruefully. "Too good, I'm afraid, after such a long time."

Reluctantly, he loosened her fingers that had, with the most delicate of tugging motions, been generating an unbearable level of sexual tension. Bringing her hand to his lips, he kissed her palm and played his tongue across her fingertips before returning it to the less volatile area of his chest. Reaching down, he cupped the back of her knee, bending it toward him, and then stroking up and down the length of her thigh.

With each stroke he ventured higher until his big hand was smoothing the soft curve of her bottom, his fingers moving over her in an intimate caress Laurel found wildly exciting. She pressed her face to his chest with a low moan that was choked off in a sharp intake of breath as her hips were suddenly arched against his. His arousal beat against the silky skin of her stomach, a hot, insistent echo of the growing demands of her own body.

They lay side by side, their bodies pressed together until with a gentle nudge Sawyer rolled her onto her back. Heeding his silent urging, Laurel parted her legs for him and discovered the magic he'd worked until now was nothing compared to the sensations that ripped through her body as his rough fingertips trailed across the sensitive flesh of her inner thighs, sliding inexorably toward his ultimate goal.

When he reached the moist, silky center of her passion, she trembled, her eyes drifting shut and a soft, exquisite sound of pleasure wafting up to stroke Sawyer's senses to an even more fevered pitch. He'd go crazy if he had to wait much longer. The warm, damp evidence that she was ready for him nearly drove him over the edge of his control. Parting her more fully, his fingers gentle and unhurried, he touched her with a firm pressure he hoped would make her as impatient to feel him deep inside her as he was to be there. The restless twitches of her hips as he kept up the tender assault told him that he'd succeeded.

It wasn't until he'd rolled to cover her with his body that Laurel felt a latent burst of panic. Instinctively, her legs clamped together and her hands shot up to ward him off. Sawyer lifted his head, surprise piercing the sensual daze that darkened his eyes to blue-black smoke.

"Laurel . . . ?" His voice was pitched low, bewildered. He searched her face as she lay silently beneath him. "What's the matter?"

Suspended between frustration and panic, she just shook her head.

Slowly his impatient look gave way to one of disbelief. "You're not . . . ?"

He firmly nudged her thighs wider apart and pressed against her, feeling her stubbornly resisting flesh and answering his own question.

"Oh, sweetheart," he groaned in a voice aching with tenderness. "Why didn't you tell me?"

"How should I know? Everything happened so fast ... and I never expected things to go this far. Besides," she added with a rueful shrug, "at my age how do you up and tell a man that ..."

"That you're a virgin?" Sawyer supplied. There was an unmistakable note of satisfaction lurking behind his indulgent smile. "I'm not sure. It's been a long time since I was on the receiving end of such an announcement. It raises an interesting point, though."

He reached for his jeans pocket and produced a small foil packet. "I wondered if I would need this."

Laurel nodded in response to his questioning look. Lord, he had addled her senses so she hadn't even thought of protection. What if ... she began to think, but resolutely shoved the thought aside. Enough of their lives had been wasted because of her preoccupation with what ifs and if onlys. No matter what tomorrow brought, she wanted this night with Sawyer.

Impulsively, she brought his mouth down to hers and poured all her desire into a deep soul-shattering kiss. Shifting her legs restlessly, she discovered that he wanted her every bit as urgently as he had a moment ago, and with an insinuating rocking movement of her hips, Laurel signaled that she was just as ready.

Sawyer broke the kiss with a ragged breath. "Sweetheart, slow down," he urged. "I should take more time ..."

"No." Laurel's head twisted on the pillow. "Love me now, Sawyer, please. Don't make me wait."

As Laurel had hoped, her plea tumbled his shaky self-control. With a rough sigh that misted her ear with heat, he positioned himself between her thighs.

"Hold me," he whispered.

Laurel obeyed, curling her fingers around his shoulders, then clenching them deeply into his hard flesh as he pressed into her. She'd thought she was prepared for the tearing stab of pain, but a small gasp escaped anyway. The next instant he came to rest deep inside her and the discomfort gradually dissolved into a warm, increasingly pleasurable feeling of fullness.

"I'm sorry, love," he whispered, brushing her eyelids with his lips. "I never want to hurt you."

"It doesn't hurt now. It feels good." She moved experimentally, a little amazed to discover that it was true. "It feels very good, actually."

"It'll get better," Sawyer promised, his lips straying to nibble her throat and the delicate curve of her ear. "I'll see to that."

He started to move inside her, slowly, deeply, and, closing her eyes, Laurel surrendered to an increasingly complex string of sensual signals. She was drifting, floating on rolling waves of pleasure that made every part of her body feel supersensitive, as if it were being stroked by a giant feather.

The pleasure gradually intensified, building, sharpening into a quest for fulfillment. Laurel wrapped her legs around him in an instinctive effort to capture more of him inside her. Her fingers raked urgently over his back, and her hips lifted and fell in time with the driving rhythm set by Sawyer. The sliding contact of their chests, slick with his sweat and hers, added to her excitement, making her ache for something that seemed just out of reach.

Laurel knew what should happen now. And she knew from Sawyer's clenched jaw and ragged breaths what it was costing him to hold back, waiting for her to climax before he let himself go.

Weaving her fingers through his hair, she kissed the side of his throat, finding the warm, salty taste of him was as stirring to her thrumming senses as his touch. "Sawyer, I don't think I can . . . I mean, this is the first time . . . it's all right if—"

"Shhh," he interrupted. "It is all right. Trust me." Grasping her hips with both hands, he withdrew, overriding her cry of protest with another firm, "Trust me," as he rolled her onto her stomach. Gently he eased a pillow beneath her hips, then entered her once more, his slow, deep strokes quickly quelling her panic.

"Trust me," he murmured a third time, slipping his hand beneath her to tease the throbbing points of her breasts before sliding over her belly and lower to find the liquid fire that engulfed him.

He rubbed her delicately at first, a gentle scraping with his fingertips that contrasted wildly with the deep thrusts of his hips. Laurel trembled under the explosive combination of sensations his body was creating in hers. Then, with a clever, intimate touch, he sent her vaulting over the top of that precipice she'd been struggling to reach. She was trembling, twisting as one after another passionate convulsion ripped through her body.

Distantly she heard his own cry of release, and knew Sawyer was falling with her as she tumbled through the darkness on the other side. It seemed to take an eternity for the millions of shimmering fragments she had exploded into to drift back together. Then, through the sensual daze that enveloped her, Laurel was pierced by a single, crystal thought—that for the first time in years she was truly whole.

She didn't open her eyes when Sawyer rolled off of her, shifting so they were in a more comfortable position with Laurel cradled against his side, her head pillowed by his damp chest.

Not until she felt the tension in his arms as he asked in a voice that sounded too casual to be casual, "Are you happy, Laurel?" did she rouse herself enough to speak.

Even then, it was only a drowsy, "Mmmm."

"No regrets?"

She smiled against his chest. Fancy Sawyer Gates having second thoughts.

"Only one." Laurel lifted her head to look at him, her smile radiant enough to chase the shadow of alarm from his eyes. "That we didn't do this years ago."

The first thing Laurel was aware of when she awoke the next morning was that she was naked beneath the sheet and blanket covering her. The second thought was that she wasn't alone.

Both were decidedly out-of-the-ordinary developments in her well-ordered life, and unexpected changes in routine were not among her favorite things. Invariably they created problems. Opening her eyes to the sight of Sawyer's head on the pillow beside hers, Laurel sleepily predicted that as problems went, he was going to be a beauty.

His hair was sticking out in a hundred different directions, a dark stubble covered his cheeks, and his mouth was slightly open, accounting for the soft, raspy breathing that had awoken her. All in all, he looked gorgeous and endearingly young in the light of early morning and even more desirable to her than he had last night. None of which changed his high ranking on the problem scale one iota.

As gingerly as possible, Laurel extricated herself from his arms and stood, only to discover that her body ached in places she'd been blissfully unaware of before last night. That wasn't surprising, of course, considering the strenuous bouts of activity she'd subjected it to between dusk and dawn. The memory alone brought a warm flush to her skin, which she quickly covered with a terry-cloth robe on her way to the kitchen.

Without thinking, she measured coffee and water into the coffeemaker, swallowed a vitamin, and made her sleepy way to the shower. It was the blast of luke-warm water that finally jarred her to full alertness, and then the magnitude of what she had done settled around her like a million sticks of dynamite, fuses lit, just wait-ing to explode.

When she'd told Sawyer last night that she didn't regret making love with him, it had been the truth . . . at the time. Technically, she supposed, it was still true, in spite of the pain in her muscles and in other more vul-nerable spots. What she did regret, wholeheartedly, was adding yet another twist to the already confusing maze of her life. Where did she go from here?

Sex with Sawyer had been glorious, surpassing even her wildest fantasies. Unfortunately, things would be much easier for her if it hadn't been. Then she could dismiss her feelings for him as a nostalgic urge to re-capture the glory of her youth and go on with her life in peace. The alternative—to admit that there had been much more to last night than a long overdue celebration of hormones—was scary. It would mean an irrevocable accounting with her past, which, in turn, could well mean giving up everything in the present and future that she'd worked so hard to get.

That was something Laurel was not prepared to do on the basis of one night in bed. She, who never so much as bought a new suit without careful forethought about how it would integrate with the rest of her ward-robe, would have to think long and hard before she tossed away the last eleven years of her life. It was bad enough that she'd risked it the way she had. She should have thought first and played later . . . if she played at all.

Well, it was too late to change that. All she could do now was minimize the damage and avoid future risks. The first step in doing that, she thought, quietly bringing her clothes into the bathroom to dress, was not to spend any more time alone with Sawyer. Especially not in a room dominated by an unmade bed and memories that were still steaming.

Chapter Six

DRESSED IN A crisp linen blazer of beige awning stripes over a slim beige skirt and silk blouse, Laurel once more looked like the woman she wanted to be: confident, composed, and in control of every detail of her existence. Hopefully, once she got to her office and saw that image reflected in the eyes of others, she would begin to feel that way again.

Things were in full chaotic swing by the time she arrived at the Department of State offices on C Street an unprecedented hour and a half late. Laurel's assistant, Jane Thomas, a slender woman in her thirties, glanced up in surprise as she strode past her desk with a distracted, "Good morning."

"Laurel?" she exclaimed, flipping a wayward curl of short brown hair off her forehead. "What are you doing here?"

"I work here. Remember?"

Jane didn't reply, but Laurel caught the way her

brows lifted in amazement at her boss's curt remark, and she drew to a halt outside the door of her corner office. Damn. She was going to have to remember that it was Sawyer whom she should be venting her irritation on, not any of her valued, extremely loyal staff.

"Jane, I'm sorry," she said, turning back to her with a grimace of self-reproach. "I don't know what's the matter with me this morning."

That wasn't quite true, but she was hardly about to air the colorful truth right here in the office.

"No problem," Jane countered. "I was just surprised to see you. When you weren't here on time, we assumed you were playing tour guide again today. Bill told us what you were doing," she explained.

"No. I just . . . overslept."

"Judging from your mood," the other woman observed, "I'd say you could have used another couple of hours. I gather you don't plan on taking up the tour business on a full-time basis?"

Laurel shook her head with a vengeance Jane couldn't possibly understand. "Not a chance."

"Good," Jane countered, standing. "Because we were lost without you. Do you by any chance have the itinerary for James Jackson's visit next month?"

"Yes. I took it home to review over the weekend."

"Did you find any problems?"

Laurel frowned. "Actually, I didn't have a chance to look at it."

"That's all right. I've already double-checked it myself. I thought it might be a good first project for Cassie . . . you know, making reservations and calling to confirm appointments."

"Cassie?" Laurel repeated, straining to attach some significance to the vaguely familiar name. Everything seemed to be a little out of focus this morning.

"Cassie Edwards," supplied Jane. "You remember, our new intern. She started yesterday."

"Of course." The intern program was a pet project of Laurel's, and it added to her feelings of disjointedness that it had so completely slipped her mind. "I'd like to meet Cassie. Where is she now?"

"Photocopying. I gave her that huge pile marked 'Someday When I Have Time I'm Going To Make A Copy Of This.'" Her lips pursed in a slightly guilty smile. "I think she'll be down there for a while."

"Slave driver," Laurel teased. "Well, if she ever re-surfaces, let me know so we can have a chat."

"Will do. Oh, and Laurel . . ."

She turned back again.

"The itinerary," Jane reminded her. "Where is it?"

"In my briefcase," Laurel replied, then glanced down in disgust at the small leather purse that was the only thing in her hands.

"Which is?" prodded Jane helpfully.

With a sigh, she answered, "At home on my desk. I'm sorry, Jane. I'll have to bring it in tomorrow."

"No problem. I'm sure I can find something else for her to do."

"Thanks."

Laurel could feel Jane's curious gaze boring into her back as she retreated to her office. No wonder. It wasn't like Laurel to completely forget about new interns and important itineraries. But then, it wasn't like her to spend impassioned, sleepless nights in the arms of an old flame either. Damn Sawyer Gates . . . and her own disgusting lack of resistance to him.

Resolutely she picked up a folder containing corre-spondence, determined to put Sawyer and last night out of her mind for the rest of the day. A little breather would probably give her new insight into the problem. And a little distance from Sawyer should certainly help put the seemingly unsurpassable splendor of last night into better perspective.

After reading the first letter in the folder three times without digesting a word, she was forced to accept the fact that she wasn't quite the master of mind control she liked to think. Faced with a subject as tempting as Sawyer, her mind was rebelling wildly against her best attempts to steer it in a more calming direction.

And Laurel knew why. She could hardly get the man out of her thoughts when she knew that at any moment he might call, demanding to speak with her or, worse, appear here in her office in the flesh. All demoralizing six feet of him. It was like waiting for the other shoe to drop. Slipping out of her apartment this morning without facing him had simply been the most sensible thing to do . . . all things considered. But in her heart, Laurel knew that Sawyer wouldn't see it that way. No, he was going to accuse her of running away again. And he was going to be very, very angry. It was no wonder she spent the rest of the morning jumping from task to task, reading reports and attending meetings in an effort to catch up, all without accomplishing a thing.

It was after lunch — a lunch eaten at her desk in order to stay close to the phone — when she finally had time to invite Cassie Edwards into her office to get acquainted. Sawyer still hadn't called, and Laurel had to admit she was beginning to feel curious — and even a little irritated. It wasn't as if she was some call girl he'd picked up in a bar, for heaven's sake; he could at least call and say . . . something.

Cassie seemed a little nervous at being summoned to the boss's office. Watching the younger woman's hands move from gripping the arms of the leather chair to twisting the soft, floral cotton of her skirt, Laurel did her best to hide her own restlessness in order to put her at ease. Cassie was tall and slender, with pale skin and auburn hair that held the promise of maturing into strik-

ing beauty one day. For now she was at that same awkward in-between age Laurel had been at when she'd left
home—sometimes gawky, sometimes graceful.

After only a few moments of conversation, Laurel
decided she liked her . . . and, she suspected, for the
same reason she liked all the interns she chose to spend
a summer working in Washington, getting a firsthand
look at the many opportunities in government. In a way,
Cassie reminded Laurel of herself, or maybe more accu-
rately, of Pandora Milinkus. Not only did she come
from a similarly underprivileged background, she was
also a walking contradiction, much as Laurel had once
been: eager and yet insecure, full of enthusiastic
dreams, but not quite sure how to pursue them.

But, if Laurel had her way, Cassie would leave here
in September with a better idea of where she was going
and with the confidence to handle head-on and intelli-
gently whatever obstacles or injustices she encountered
along the way. It was a lesson which could have
changed Laurel's life if she'd learned it sooner, and regret that she hadn't gave her special energy and patience
in dealing with young people like Cassie who could still
avoid making the kind of desperate mistake she had.

"Remember, Cassie," Laurel told the young woman
after they'd talked for a while, "if you have any questions at all, just ask—me, Jane, whoever's around at
the moment. That's the only way you're going to learn."

Cassie returned her smile, looking considerably less
intimidated than she had when she first sat down. "I'll
try. But everyone always looks so busy. I hate to bother
anyone."

"It's no bother. We work as a team around here, Cassie, and now you're part of it. If you have a question—
or a problem—I want to hear about it." She stood,
accompanying the younger woman to the office door.

"Thanks, Ms. Forr . . . Laurel," Cassie corrected herself, remembering Laurel's request that she use her first name. "I just know this summer is going to be great."

"I hope so, Cassie." Laurel grinned. "Just don't get so caught up in your work here that you forget to have some fun."

Cassie accepted the lighthearted advice with a laugh and headed back to the desk she'd been given on the other side of the department's outer office.

"Words of wisdom if ever I heard them. Too bad you're not smart enough to practice what you preach."

The other shoe. Laurel would recognize that dry, gritty voice anywhere, and she took care to clear her expression of any trace of the foolish excitement that raced through her at the sound of it before turning to face Sawyer.

He was leaning against the outer wall of her office, his arms folded across his chest, and he was in rather a testy mood if she was any interpreter of male body language. Hair combed, cheeks shaved, and clad in a steel gray suit that fit his lean, angular body with hand-tailored precision, he looked wonderful. Laurel controlled the urge to tell him so.

"What are you doing here?" she demanded.

"Visiting."

Straightening, he shoved his hands in his pants pockets and ambled into her office, plopping down in the chair in front of her desk as if invited. Laurel followed him in, none too pleased by the nonchalant way he was assuming she had time to waste on him.

"I'm really very busy this afternoon," she ventured, remaining standing behind the solid leather barrier of her chair. No need to encourage his lingering. "Did you want something special?"

She could have choked on the words as a suggestive gleam lit his eyes even before she'd finished speaking. Mercifully, though, he let it go at that.

"As a matter of fact, yes. I overheard your kind

words to . . . Cassie, was it? Anyway, it so happens *I* have a question . . . and a problem. Want to hear them?"

"No."

"No?" He feigned surprise. "Why not?"

"Because I'm busy."

A smile lifted one corner of his mouth as he gazed at the perfectly clear top of her desk, his comment silent but eloquent. "What happened to teamwork and all that?"

"It still exists. You just don't happen to be on the team."

Her triumphant smile wilted quickly under the heat of his gaze.

"That's not how it felt last night," he murmured. "I thought we made a pretty terrific team. World class, in fact." He snapped his fingers. "You've got connections; maybe you could see about getting a new event added to the Olympics—sexual endurance. Dane could even run an editorial—"

"Stop," Laurel ordered. Jasper and sex and Sawyer and her all tangled in the same conversation was too much to handle. She could actually feel the pink creeping across her cheeks. "This is hardly the proper place to exchange childish, sexual innuendoes."

"True," he agreed with exaggerated remorse. "You should have hung around this morning so we could have exchanged them properly . . . in the sack."

Laurel's palm slapped the high chair back. "I knew it. I knew that's what was bothering you. You're angry because I left before you woke up this morning."

"Quiet, Laurel," Sawyer admonished, grinning like a man without a care in the world. "Do you want your whole staff to think I'm easy?"

Lord, she'd been practically shouting. The pink in her cheeks burst into flames that quickly spread down her throat.

"And besides," he continued in that same damn casual tone, "I'm not angry at you for running out on me. I expected it."

"Don't start."

"After all, it's not easy breaking old habits. I'll bet that last night was the first time in years you did something because you wanted to, not because it was part of some master plan."

"You're crazy."

"It's understandable that you'd backslide a bit afterwards."

"I want you to leave."

"It must have been quite a shock looking yourself in the eye in the mirror this morning."

"Now."

"Tell me, did all that honesty scare the hell out of you?"

"I don't have to listen to this."

The narrow heels of her shoes stabbed the carpet with each step Laurel took toward the door. If he wouldn't leave and put an end to their ridiculous dueling conversation, she would. Then Sawyer's lazy, taunting laugh hit her like a knife between her shoulder blades, stopping her cold.

"That's right, Laurel, run. It makes things all the more interesting."

On a slow count of ten, she turned back to face him, determined to regain control of the situation. "I don't have to run, Sawyer, because you're leaving. Please don't make me have you thrown out."

"I wouldn't dream of it, darlin'," he drawled, standing and sauntering to her side. "Can you imagine what old Jasper would say if he got wind of my suffering such gross inhospitality at your hands?"

She could well imagine Jasper's shocked dismay. With a defiant toss of her head, she said, "I'm sure he would understand and support whatever course of action I felt I had to take. *Always.*"

"Ouch. Point taken, honey." He chucked her under her upthrust chin. "Fortunately, what you lack in subtlety you make up for in . . . other ways. If you didn't, I might lose interest in this little reunion of ours."

Laurel slapped his hand away, infuriated by his insolent attitude. "The reunion is over," she snapped. "You can mark whatever debt you *think* I owed you paid in full."

The smile left his face and sparks of the anger she'd sensed earlier lit his eyes.

"Your debt is paid when I say it's paid," he said quietly, his voice as unyielding as cold-forged steel.

Amidst her irritation with him, Laurel felt a curious tug of relief that he wasn't going to permit her to sweep him from her life so easily. No matter what she told him—or herself—the truth was that she didn't know what she wanted. It was like being at an unfamiliar crossroads without any signposts or map to warn what lay ahead in either direction. It was unnerving.

"I really don't have time to waste discussing this," she informed him, waving her hand toward the door in a gesture that clearly said he was to leave.

Sawyer surprised her by agreeing. "It's just as well." With a quick glance at his watch, he added, "I have to be at the airport in less than an hour to pick up Maureen." He looked at her blandly. "You remember I told you about Maureen Dakin? One of my partners?"

"Vaguely," she murmured. Questions about why Maureen Dakin was joining him in Washington and the full scope of the business they were engaged in together were suddenly running with high voltage through her body. "Well, you better be shoving off," she advised before she weakened and asked them. "I certainly wouldn't want you to keep your partner waiting. And next time," she added, "call me before you decide to *visit*."

"Oh, I wasn't here to visit you," Sawyer returned,

his expression of innocent surprise striking a suspicious chord in Laurel. "Didn't I mention that I dropped by to see Bill Reynolds?"

"No," she replied, mimicking his mild tone. "You didn't."

The smile that lifted the corners of his mouth was decidedly mocking. "It must have slipped my mind."

"I'll bet."

"At any rate, I stopped by to see if I could wrangle an invitation to this evening's reception for some visiting British diplomats."

"And could you?"

"Yes. Your boss graciously agreed to include me. I'm looking forward to getting some firsthand British reaction to my proposal."

She tried hard not to grit her teeth. "How nice."

"Personally I would have chosen . . . *interesting* as a better word to describe this evening." He emphasized the undercurrents in his remark by reaching out and quickly—before Laurel could gather words for a protest—sliding his thumb across her bottom lip, managing to make the light caress intimate by stroking deeply enough to tease the soft, damp flesh inside.

"I'll see you there, darlin'," he promised silkily, then disappeared, leaving Laurel awash in conflicting emotions.

Of course, Sawyer would have to know that Jasper, and therefore she, too, would be present at the informal affair to be held in one of the diplomatic reception rooms on the eighth floor. She had already received the inevitable call from Jasper's secretary, reminding her that he would meet her there at five on the dot. She'd been wanting to capitalize on a low-level headache and beg off—now she longed to do so even more . . . but at the same time she couldn't curb a flutter of anticipation.

In just a few hours she would be with Sawyer again. No, she thought, horrified by the mental blunder. She

would be with Jasper, and most likely struggling to balance the two very different men like a juggler working
with a watermelon and a crystal vase. Her headache was
suddenly no longer low-level.

"Laurel, I'd like to speak with you if you have a
minute."

Bill Reynolds was standing in the doorway. Behind
heavy black-rimmed glasses his eyes were troubled, and
Laurel felt instant alarm. Bill usually sailed through
even the direst catastrophes with a smile.

"Sure, Bill. Would you like to sit down?"

He shook his head. "No, I still have a few more calls
to make, but I thought you should know about this right
away. I haven't been able to get through to Jasper."

"What is it?"

"It's about this Gates fellow. I have a source over in
Mike Riordon's office, and he overheard an interesting
conversation between the senator and Gates earlier
today."

Laurel didn't even blink at the mention of how Bill
had obtained his information. She'd learned early on
that sources and leaks—both secret and not so secret—
were just one more wheel in the gears of political life.
What did concern her was that this particular tidbit involved Sawyer.

"What sort of conversation?" she asked.

"About Jasper. It's no secret that Jasper has long-
standing friendships with some of the most powerful oil
men in the country. Naturally their interests often con-
flict with those of an entrepreneur like Gates."

"Jasper is aware of that. I'm sure that's why he made
a special effort to be hospitable to Mr. Gates." At my
expense, thought Laurel. For the first time she was feeling the strain of the role she'd chosen to play.

"I know. That's why I agreed to include him in tonight's reception. But that was before I spoke with my
friend. I think Jasper is under the impression that Gates

is only here to check him out, to find out where he stands on certain issues. But I'm afraid that's not the case," Bill revealed with obvious concern.

"What do you mean?"

"Gates's mind is already made up on the matter. He's here for one reason only, and that's to do whatever he can to stop Jasper from becoming ambassador."

"Are you sure?" Laurel's brow wrinkled as she tried to remember if Sawyer had said—or worse, asked—any questions of her that would bear out what Bill was suggesting.

Bill nodded. "I've just finished doing some further checking on my own, and there's no question about it. Gates's company has both feet in a prospective deal to join forces with a British oil company in developing leases in the North Sea. That isn't going to sit well with some of the big U.S. oil companies. The deal is risky as it is. Naturally, Gates doesn't want to take a chance on Jasper siding with his friends and doing something diplomatically to sour it."

"So you think he's trying to influence Mike Riordon to vote against Jasper's confirmation?"

"I think he's already got Riordon in his pocket. What he wants now is for Riordon to influence others on the committee. And if what my friend overheard is true, he's found the ammunition to do it."

All the color seemed to drain from the world around her. Inside and out, everything turned the cold gray shade of dread.

"What sort of ammunition?" she forced herself to ask.

"That I don't know exactly. Only that it's some kind of sensitive background information guaranteed to blow Jasper right out of the water politically. Gates's partner is evidently flying in sometime today for the kill."

Laurel grimaced. The kill. How apropos. Soon, now, Laurel Forrest would be publicly and professionally, if not literally, dead. Fighting through a backwash of panic and bitterness, she searched for an appropriate response to present to Bill.

"Jasper will have to be told as soon as possible," he was saying urgently.

"Of course, he'll have to be told." Laurel bit her lip in thought and was rewarded as the thread of an idea that just might save her tickled the edges of her mind. "But maybe not as soon as possible."

Laurel spoke quickly and somehow managed to convince Bill that it wasn't in Jasper's best interest to dump all this on him right before this evening's reception. It would only serve to upset him. Far better if she were the one to break the bad news later, when they were alone. Then he would have time to contemplate his next move. Perhaps in the meantime, she suggested, she could even speak to Gates privately and find out a little more about what he knew and what he planned to do with the information. In a roundabout way, of course.

By the time Bill left her office, patting her chummily on the shoulder for exhibiting such good sense, Laurel felt as if she had run a marathon. And the real test was still ahead.

Compared to Sawyer, manipulating Bill Reynolds had been only a foot race.

Chapter Seven

DULLES INTERNATIONAL AIRPORT, where Maureen was scheduled to arrive, was located twenty-five miles west of downtown Washington. With the late-afternoon traffic leaving the city, it would probably take him at least an hour to get there, but Sawyer didn't care. He had a lot on his mind, and he did some of his best thinking behind the wheel of a car.

It was a habit that had been forged when he was still a teenager and his car had been his only means of escape. Hanging around home had invariably meant being assigned another chore from his father's endless list. He had never minded the work, whether it was stocking shelves at the store or swinging a hammer on one of the boats his father repaired on the side. What he'd hated was having every minute of the day planned for him, as if to imply that, left to his own devices, he'd end up in trouble.

Which is exactly what his father had feared most. No

son of his was going to hang around on a street corner. Hard work was what it took to make a man. A man got the job done right and he got it done fast . . . and he didn't look for a pat on the back for doing what he was supposed to do in the first place. Convinced that coddling was what turned boys into sissies, the elder Gates hadn't been very free with either compliments or affection. And Sawyer's mother, raised in a small Mexican village, wasn't one to question what the man of the house decreed.

After a while Sawyer had stopped knocking himself out trying to earn a word of praise from his father and had simply done what was required of him. And whenever he'd needed some time alone, he'd invented an excuse involving either school or football—the only two activities outside of work that were legitimate in his father's view—and had taken off in the car he'd had to fight to buy with his own money.

How he'd loved that old '62 Chevy convertible. It might not have had air conditioning or a computerized dashboard, but it had been every bit as comfortable and powerful as the fancy rented Cadillac he was now driving. And it hadn't had a scratch on it either, until that night a few months after Dory left when he'd driven it into the garage and straight on through the back wall. His mood that night had been six parts anger and frustration and four parts beer. Afterward, he hadn't even bothered getting an estimate on the repairs needed. He'd simply called a junkyard owner to haul the car away—putting an end to the chapter of his life in which it had played such an integral part.

Only it hadn't worked out that way.

Oh, sure, he'd stopped spending his evenings trying in vain to drown his sorrows with Coors and had gotten on with the business of living his life. Except that it had never felt exactly like *living* after Dory left. It had felt more like settling for what was left. Actually, in some ways, he'd been living more freely than he ever had, taking whatever risk came along—business-related and otherwise—without much thought of the consequences. He wasn't inclined toward introspection, but occasionally it hit him that he was a walking fulfillment of that line in the old Kristofferson song: He'd found a kind of freedom, yes—but only because he had nothing left to lose . . .

He'd been telling the truth last night when he'd told Laurel that what they'd shared had never really ended for him. Always it had loomed just on the outskirts of reality, a murky collage of memories and pain which he refused to examine too closely. Seeing her again had simply focused a spotlight on it, peeling away the layers of insulation, and suddenly the past had come rushing to the surface.

Outwardly, Dory had had next to nothing going for her when they'd first met. Hell, even though they went to the same relatively small high school, Sawyer had never even noticed her before that day he almost ran her over. But right from the start he'd felt linked to her on a level he'd never even approached with any other woman before or since. It had nothing to do with the way she dressed or where she lived—although he'd had the devil's own time convincing her of that.

Life up until that point had done an A-1 job of teaching her otherwise, of demonstrating in cruel detail that those things were all that did matter and that she didn't come close to having what it took. For starters she'd been saddled with that nightmare of a name—Pandora Milinkus—and a father who was usually as drunk and abusive as Sawyer's was relentlessly hard driving. And, like his own mother, hers had provided precious little in the way of an emotional buffer.

But all of that had ceased to matter when they came together. Maybe they'd each recognized the search for acceptance and approval in the other, and that had made it easier to fulfill each other's needs. But, whatever the reason, Laurel had become his whole world. And suddenly everything else had seemed just filler, taking up whatever time surrounded the hours when they could be together. Attuned to the desperation in her need to get away from home, he had made her dreams his own. All he'd really needed to be happy was Dory, but if her happiness depended on getting as far away from Beaumont as she could, then he'd been equally determined to make it happen.

His father's death had changed all that, although at first Sawyer hadn't realized just how completely. Naively, he'd assumed that loving him the way she claimed to, Dory would put their plans on hold until he could make some arrangements for his family's support. He'd never felt anything close to the tangle of emotions that swept through him when it finally penetrated his thick skull that she wasn't going to wait. Pain, frustration, confusion, anger . . . fury, really, so cold and deep that it had driven him closer to an act of violence than at any other time in his life. It had brought him within a heartbeat of claiming in anger all the love Dory had been withholding until they were married.

In his pain, her holding back had seemed like the ultimate betrayal. He'd felt like a fool for dancing to her tune for so long—and he'd had to reach deep inside for the self-control to stop short of raping her. He hadn't been a gentleman about it, either. He'd shoved her from the car, telling her to go ahead and leave, that he was well rid of such a lying tease. It had been a long, long time before he'd stopped aching enough to feel sorry for that last bit of cruelty.

This morning when he'd awoken to find Laurel gone, he'd felt a pale echo of that long-ago pain and frustration. Even with eleven added years of wisdom and experience under his belt, it had taken him most of the morning to shake the feeling of betrayal and admit that it was natural for her to react as skittishly as she had. He supposed it was unrealistic to expect that last night would have sealed things for her as completely as it had for him. The important thing was that when he did manage to get past her slick veneer of defenses, the woman trusted him. He would just have to build on that.

As a first step in that direction, he'd planned to nurture her trust by returning the favor and coming clean about his reason for being in Washington. Then, when he'd stopped by her office earlier, she'd rubbed his ego the wrong way by not being overcome with pleasure—and somehow they'd gotten entangled in another round of verbal one-upmanship.

Maybe it was just as well, he decided, parking the car and checking the overhead monitor for the gate number. It might be wiser to wait and tell Laurel everything after the fact. After all, he still had to convince Maureen that he was handling this the right way, and one contrary female at a time was enough to handle.

Not surprisingly to Sawyer, Maureen was the first passenger to disembark, her stride long and purposeful. Hurrying to his side, she stretched one arm around his neck in a perfunctory hug and pecked his cheek with a kiss. Beneath the hurried affection, Sawyer could feel her agitation, and he attempted to postpone the inevitable showdown until they were alone by paying her a compliment.

Running his gaze with quick approval over her sleek blond hairdo and a figure that was—to her great consternation—softly rounded, he drawled, "You look great, Maureen. You won't even have to change for the reception . . . which is fortunate because we're running late. Is that a new dress?"

She glanced quickly, pointedly, at the teal silk shirtwaist. "No, it's a very old dress. And a very old line. So, save it, Sawyer. I'm not going to be charmed or distracted into forgetting what I flew all this way to ask you."

"That's what I like about you, partner," Sawyer countered, commandeering her carry-on bag. "You've got determination." He started walking. "The car's this way. Did I mention that the one I rented just happens to be your favorite color? It's a—"

"Sawyer," Maureen broke in. She hadn't taken a step and didn't sound as if she was about to.

Sawyer stopped, turning back to her with a sigh. "Go ahead, Maureen. Ask."

Stepping quickly to his side, Maureen glared at him with that wild-eyed expression she always wore when profits were involved. Her voice reminded him of a cat's hiss as she demanded, "Have you completely lost your mind?"

"I hope not," Sawyer retorted, his smile grim.

"Then I can't understand why you've decided to do what you have. A very important project is at stake here, Sawyer . . . and lots and lots of cold, hard cash. One-third of which, if I might be so tactless to remind you, has my name on it. You're the one who was so hot to trot on this idea from the start, and now you're about to put it all on the line? Without, I might add, a thought for all the weeks and weeks of preparation involved and the up-front expenses, and all for God knows what reason?"

"I told you on the phone this morning, Maureen, the reason is a personal matter."

"Well, the result will be a decidedly impersonal matter. It will be a business matter—one that could cost all of us a small fortune."

"I've already made up my mind, Maureen, and I've cleared it with Reece."

"Reece," she scoffed. "He's so busy chasing his secretary around her desk that half the time he doesn't know what he's approving. At least, thank God, I don't have to worry about skirt-chasing interfering with your business sense—" She broke off with a sudden, horrified frown as she caught his self-deprecatory grimace. "Tell me this isn't because of a woman. Tell me, Sawyer," she prodded impatiently.

In a monotone he parroted, "This isn't because of a woman."

"Now tell me the truth."

"This isn't about a woman . . . exactly."

"What on earth does that mean?"

"It means, it's personal. Look, Maureen, together Reece and I can override your vote, but I don't want it to be that way. That's why I didn't argue when you insisted on flying out here. I thought it might be easier to explain this to you in person. But it isn't." He shrugged wearily. "Hell, I'm not even sure I understand myself all that's happening. But I'm asking you as a partner and as a friend to let me run with the ball on this one."

Maureen scoured his face in silence. Searching, Sawyer supposed, for the explanations she knew better than to try and wheedle out of him. He could feel the war going on inside her head as hundreds of travelers detoured around them. He only hoped the friendship that had grown between them since Dak's death would win out over her fierce drive to win at any cost.

"All right," she said finally, her smile grudging, but signaling, Sawyer knew, that she was with him. "It's all yours." She held out the slim leather briefcase she was carrying. "In here is all the background information you requested. It took me most of the night, but I was able to document everything you told me. I just hope you know what you're doing."

"So do I, pal," Sawyer muttered under his breath as he clamped the briefcase under his arm and started toward the car once more. "So do I."

* * *

By the time Sawyer and Maureen arrived at the stately room where the reception was being held, Laurel had already been there, clutching a glass of wine and the same swan-shaped cheese puff to keep from biting her perfectly manicured nails, for an hour. In a brainstorm born of anxiety, she'd asked Jane and Cassie to be on hand for the reception, insisting it was never too soon for Cassie to witness firsthand the result of all their planning and strategy.

Ordinarily, Laurel had no problem combining her obligations to Jasper with her responsibilities as unofficial hostess at affairs such as this one. But tonight she didn't feel up to monitoring the mountains of hors d'oeuvres and rivers of alcohol required even for what was a small crowd by Washington standards . . . fewer than one hundred guests. Fortunately, Jane had stepped in to handle all that without a single word about the uncharacteristically frazzled state of her boss, leaving Laurel free to circulate—and to keep a wary eye on the door.

She was in the middle of introducing Cassie to some other State Department employees, careful to stay close enough to the entrance to monitor the late arrivals without being so close as to be taken by surprise, when Sawyer walked in. Laurel didn't recognize the woman by his side—she'd been half afraid another ghost from her past might appear—but assumed she must be his partner, Maureen Dakin. What she did recognize was the type. A glamorous blonde, impeccably tanned from her smooth forehead to her no doubt painted toenails, Maureen Dakin was the type who eleven years ago had spent Saturday afternoons dressed in a cutely scant outfit, turning cartwheels by the edge of the football field while Sawyer scored touchdowns. Laurel had spent those afternoons helping her mother clean other people's houses for extra money.

Suddenly, she could feel the mouse brown of her hair

smothering any trace of golden and amber highlights and the scattering of freckles across her nose growing bolder until they stood out like warts against her pale skin. Obviously, Sawyer recognized her in spite of the transformation, and she watched with a sinking feeling of dread as he grasped Maureen's elbow and steered her in Laurel's direction.

Quickly ditching the swan cheese puff, she tried to look as nonchalant as possible as she smoothed her hair, which today hung loose to her shoulders. Despite her still attentive expression, she'd somehow lost all sense of what Cassie was saying to her.

Why, oh, *why* hadn't she remembered that tonight was the British reception when she was getting dressed this morning? The embarrassingly obvious answer to that question was still bearing down on her with a determined gleam in his eye. If she had remembered, she would definitely have worn something less businesslike, less stiff, less *beige*, for pity's sake. She would have worn something soft and clingy and teal blue . . .

"Hello, Laurel. I'd like you to meet Maureen Dakin, one of my business partners. Maureen, this is . . . Laurel Forrest. Laurel's with the State Department, and she's also a friend of Jasper Dane."

Laurel conjured up a small insincere smile and found a trace of irony in the fact that the other woman was obviously doing the same. As they shook hands briefly and murmured appropriate greetings, Maureen Dakin studied Laurel's face with an odd, curious expression. Laurel suddenly recognized it as one that signaled a vague stirring of memory, and, with an uneasy jolt, she tried to deflect disaster by hastily introducing Cassie.

"We've already met," Sawyer said, lifting an eyebrow in response to her fumbling introduction. "Cassie was dropping some papers off in Bill Reynolds's office this afternoon when I stopped by. It's nice to see you again, Cassie."

Laurel watched, without the slightest surprise, Cassie's flustered reaction to having Sawyer's dark eyes and slow smile unfurled on her alone. It was the invariable female response to the rough-edged charm which even as a teenager he had wielded without conscious effort. Chemistry. The man was blessed with great chemistry. And no honor, she reminded herself. Eleven years ago he had summarily destroyed the hopes and dreams that had been her life line, and now he was about to do it all over again.

"Cassie," Sawyer said in that gravelly tone that had the power to melt the sturdiest feminine constitution into a puddle of primal responses, "you've been here long enough to get the lay of the land. Would you mind showing Maureen to the buffet table?"

"Of course not," Cassie replied.

At the same instant Maureen delivered a crisp, "Thanks, I'm not hungry."

Sawyer turned to her with a steely smile. "Force yourself."

Laurel couldn't decide if the hand he placed at Maureen's waist to give her a gentle shove was friendly familiar or possessive familiar. Not that she should care, she thought, caring anyway.

"Alone at last," Sawyer drawled when the other two women had left. "Did you miss me?"

"Like a toothache."

"Aren't you afraid such lavish endearments will go to my head and I'll start taking you for granted?"

Laurel stared at him, dropping all pretense of a smile. "No, Sawyer, that's not what I'm afraid of at all."

There wasn't so much as a flicker of his straight, thick black eyelashes in response to her quiet, unmistakably pointed remark. Instead, he directed a bland gaze toward the buffet table.

"Cassie's a very pretty girl," he remarked. "She reminds me a little bit of you at her age."

"God forbid."

"Got your blinders back on, Laurel? Whether you admit it or not, you *were* pretty, even then. And smart and enthusiastic and not nearly as wary as you always seem to be these days."

"When I was her age, I was also poised on the brink of making a whopper of a mess out of my life. I hope Cassie won't be at all like me in that regard."

"Bill told me you were gung ho about this internship program," he revealed, swinging an interested gaze back at her. "Is that why, Laurel? For atonement?"

Laurel shrugged off the suggestion, which was partly truth. "Maybe I just like to see kids who ordinarily wouldn't get a break get one. If in the process I can prevent someone else from making a mistake like I did, all the better."

"Some mistakes can be undone, Laurel. Sometimes we're given a second chance to get it right."

Something seductive in the tone of his voice brought Laurel's head up sharply. "And sometimes someone else sees fit to undo our mistakes for us. Isn't that right, Sawyer?"

The look that flashed in his eyes might have been wariness, or it might have been guilt. Either way it served to confirm all her suspicions.

"I want to talk to you," she hissed.

"I thought that's what we were doing."

"I mean privately."

His smile was a wicked, fleeting twist of his lips. "Shall we look for a terrace?"

"Not this time, " snapped Laurel. "Just outside there will do nicely."

She led the way to a spot directly outside the double-doored entrance where they were out of earshot of everyone else, but by no means as isolated as they'd been the other night. Laurel whirled to face him, her expression fierce and determined.

"This afternoon you said you had a problem you wanted to discuss with me," she plunged right in. "What was it?"

Sawyer eyed her negligently. "I don't remember."

"Don't you lie to me."

"All right. I do remember. But this afternoon I was in the mood for talking. Now I'm not."

"Tough. I have some questions and this time you owe me . . . you owe me answers. The truth. Did you come to Washington expressly to stop Jasper's confirmation as ambassador?"

The only muscle in his entire body that moved was that one in his left cheek. A dead giveaway that he wasn't feeling nearly as serene as he'd obviously like Laurel to think.

"Who told you that?" he demanded quietly.

"Is it true?"

"First I want to know who told you."

Laurel hesitated, then with a shrug snapped, "Bill Reynolds. Well? Is it true?"

"It's true that's why I came to Washington," Sawyer admitted, speaking slowly, as if a great deal of thought preceded the utterance of each word.

Playing for time, Laurel thought bitterly. Time to plan his strategy, time to cover his tracks. She was determined to allow him as little as possible. She was equally determined to present her case in a controlled, dignified manner as she tried to convince him to find another means of taking his revenge on her instead of crushing a lifelong dream of Jasper's, one he deserved to have come true. But against the cold, remote look in his eyes, all her resolve and all her carefully constructed arguments were as doomed as seedlings facing an early frost.

"You bastard," she heard herself say instead of the

brilliant speech she had planned. Pain quivered in her voice. Suddenly her very real concern for Jasper and all her prudent thoughts for her own future were washed aside by the sweeping reality of his betrayal.

Sawyer gave a short, sarcastic laugh. "My, my, such touching, wifelike loyalty. And you're not even officially engaged yet. Tell me, what does the man do to earn such devotion." He hesitated before adding, "I already found out firsthand what he *doesn't* do."

Laurel would have thought she was beyond being hurt by his savage taunts. Surely the knife could only plunge so deep, twist so hard, and she was already at that point and beyond. When, she wondered wistfully, did numbness set in?

"This has nothing to do with loyalty," she insisted, fighting to control the increasingly chaotic waves of emotion inside, "or with whether or not we're officially engaged. I'm just not going to let you punish Jasper for something I did."

Sawyer slitted his eyes briefly, as if caught off guard. And even Laurel, who knew better, could have sworn it was confusion that clouded them momentarily.

"I just admitted to you that my reason for coming to Washington was to stop Dane," he reminded her. "That was before I even knew you were here. So how could my motives possibly involve you?"

"I'm not saying it started with me," explained Laurel. "But the fact is that without me you wouldn't have anything on Jasper. Once you've exposed me as a liar and a fraud, his mere association with me will be enough to make the committee question his suitability. Every reporter in town will jump on the story, and some one of them will discover that when I first arrived in Washington Jasper smoothed out a few rough spots for me. Nothing illegal, certainly nothing out of the ordinary in this town, but it will be all the leverage your buddy Riordon needs to swing votes against Jasper."

Laurel forced her voice to project a calmness she was far from feeling. "Admit it, Sawyer, you stumbled onto a golden opportunity. You get your revenge by destroying me and you knock Jasper out of the way with the same blow. It's perfect."

Now that it was out in the open, the backs of her eyelids were stinging and her breath was catching spasmodically even before Sawyer's fingers clenched around her shoulders.

"What the hell are you talking about?" he demanded.

"Don't you touch me," she cried, trying to wrench free. "Don't you ever touch me again."

"I'm going to do a hell of a lot more than touch you if you don't calm down and start making sense. I'm going to shake the answers out of you." With a short, explicit curse, he released her and dragged a clean white handkerchief from his pocket. "Here. Wipe your face."

"I don't want—"

"Tough." Knocking her hands aside, he dabbed at her cheeks with the soft cotton, his touch as gentle as his expression was violent.

"Now tell me exactly what Reynolds told you," he ordered. "Everything."

Those few seconds of silence had been enough for Laurel to begin to regain control of her emotions. She called on an old trick of focusing on getting through one moment at a time. Please, God, just this next one.

"I've already told you everything he told me," she replied. "Simply that you aren't here to check out Jasper as Riordon claimed, but to ruin his chances of being confirmed. The rest I figured out for myself. It didn't take a genius."

"Nonsense seldom does."

"Don't you dare try and deny it. I'm a fool, but not so big a one that I'd fall for your lies twice."

"And exactly what lies are those?" he inquired coldly.

Laurel wished there was some way she could shatter his icy control, but, of course, there wasn't. You had to feel something in order to be pushed to the kind of raw anger she longed to see him suffer. In spite of his performance in bed last night, she had no doubt that it had been a long, long time since Sawyer felt anything for her besides contempt . . . and maybe a little basic lust.

"Exactly what those lies were doesn't really matter," she told him. Her tone was a mixture of anger and resignation. "What matters is that you used me, Sawyer. You lied to me and let me believe that you still cared, that maybe we really could salvage something from the past. And I bought it all. You got me to drop my guard in a way I never thought I would again. I told you everything, things I knew I shouldn't tell anyone ever. I told you everything you needed to know to destroy me. God, I played right into your hands," she finished with a knife-edged laugh.

For what felt like an eternity, Sawyer stood absolutely still, not saying a word. "I see that you've given a lot of thought to this."

"As I said, it didn't take a genius to read the writing on the wall."

He nodded slowly. "There's just one little thing I don't understand."

"What's that?" Laurel didn't like the way he was acting, not at all. She wouldn't have believed a word, of course, but she'd expected him to at least attempt to deny her accusations. Or explain them away.

"I took you to bed *after* you told me about your past," he stated bluntly.

"So?"

"So, if I'd already lied and wormed what I needed to know out of you, why did I bother playing what must have been my trump card . . . sex?"

Laurel's stomach clenched. Her cheeks felt like they were on fire. "I think that's rather obvious."

"Not to me. So why don't you spell it out?"

"The sex," Laurel spoke bitterly, refusing to flinch from his sharp gaze, "was simply the icing on the cake."

"Ah, I see. Sort of a bonus."

His manner was making Laurel more and more uncomfortable. He sounded almost bored by the whole matter, but his body was sending out very different signals. Instead of his ordinarily loose stance, he gave the impression of being tightly wired, as if every muscle was tensed to the breaking point. Most disturbing of all were his eyes. They gleamed like ebony lances, pinning her to some invisible wall. Laurel relinquished all hope of trying to talk him out of what he had planned, praying only that she could somehow maneuver to minimize Jasper's losses. At this point her own future wasn't worth begging for.

"So, you're saying I came to Washington to find a way to stop Dane and lucked out by meeting up with you again?" he asked her, as if still unclear of the point she was making.

"Right. I realize, of course, that you could have blown the whistle on me that first night and embarrassed Jasper out of contention... the fact that my story only got worse and worse must have seemed too good to be true. And I also realize why you waited... you wanted to collect your pound of flesh."

She squared her shoulders to go on. "Well, you've got it, Sawyer, and now you're about to get everything else you want as well. I only have one... favor to ask of you. Let me explain everything to Jasper first... before you go to him or the newspapers or whomever it is you're planning to give the information to. That way he'll have the opportunity to withdraw from consideration on his own, instead of being publicly humiliated."

His eyes glittered with frost. "And if he does withdraw, there'll really be no need for me to expose you publicly, either. Is that the second half of the favor you're asking, Laurel?"

"Absolutely not. Do you think I'd ask you to do anything for me?" Her voice was stiff with the control it took to keep from lashing out at him. For Jasper's sake, she would play this in as civilized a manner as she could manage.

"Why not?" Sawyer retorted harshly. "It would make for a very clever, inventive solution to your problem. And you're really good at being inventive, aren't you, *Laurel?* In fact, for all I know it was *you* who was trying to use me all along, and it just backfired."

Confusion softened Laurel's frown. "I don't know what you're talking about."

"I'm talking about a 'pound of flesh,' sweetheart." His words were like daggers of ice, and after hurling them, he waited with a black smile for them to hit their mark before he continued. "All that crap about being chummy and hospitable aside, Dane knew from the start that I opposed his confirmation. Maybe you and he figured that you could find out exactly what I was up to if you got close enough to me to convince me that you still cared . . . that maybe we could salvage something from the past," he finished in a savage echo of her own words.

"My God, you really are a bastard," Laurel whispered. "How could you think that?"

"How could you?"

The impassioned tremor that ran through his deep voice caught Laurel off guard. There was a moment of frozen stillness as she stared up into his eyes. They were heavily shadowed, and his mouth had a strangely injured twist. Anxiously, she searched for signs of the smug satisfaction and triumph she'd prepared herself to endure, but instead the glittering black depths of his eyes were like mirrors, reflecting back all the aching bitterness inside her.

Without thinking, she reached out to touch his arm, but he very efficiently moved it just out of reach, leaving her feeling foolish with her hand hanging limply in midair. If he had been feeling pain a moment ago, it was now concealed behind the cool cynical look she knew so well.

"I think it's time we got back to the party," he stated.

"What . . . what about what I asked earlier?" Laurel marshaled the courage to venture. "Will you let me be the one to tell Jasper first?"

He glanced over her shoulder, a smile slowly moving across his lips. "Sure. You're about to get your chance right now."

Laurel followed his gaze and saw Jasper standing in the doorway about twenty feet away. Maureen Dakin was by his side, smiling and nodding at something he'd just said. He waved his hand for Laurel to join them.

Panic ripped through her.

"Please," she implored, turning back to Sawyer. "I need more time . . . I can't tell him like this."

He glared at her.

"Please."

"I'll think about it," he growled.

"But . . ."

His hand landed against her back, shoving her in the direction of the door and ending the discussion. Laurel felt queasy as she stood between the two men, smiling through Jasper's teasing remarks about how he seemed to be always losing her at parties lately. Maureen lifted an eyebrow at Sawyer who was standing there with an expression about as friendly as a rockslide.

"Anyway, the reason I was looking for the two of you," Jasper said, abandoning the doomed line of patter, "was to invite Sawyer to spend the weekend at the farm. It's just a little spread . . . forty acres just inside Virginia. Maureen said she'd love to come for a little swimming, a little tennis. And Laurel will be there, of course . . ."

"Actually, Jasper," Laurel interrupted, "I won't be able to get away this weekend."

"Nonsense." Jasper smiled, but he gave her a look, a very pointed look, which Laurel suddenly found maddeningly condescending. "It's Marsha's birthday on Saturday—my daughter," he explained for the benefit of Maureen and Sawyer. "I'm anxious to have my two girls get better acquainted." He gave Laurel's shoulder a quick squeeze.

Somehow she was able to resist flinching away, but when Sawyer's dark eyes rested on her, it was impossible not to squirm.

"Under the circumstances," he said, "I don't see how Laurel can possibly refuse to attend. Or myself, either, for that matter. A weekend in the country sounds like just the thing to liven up my visit East."

At first Laurel was horrified. Then the possibilities of the situation hit her. It was a reprieve of sorts. Surely Sawyer wouldn't do anything before the weekend if he planned to spend it as a guest in Jasper's home.

Three days. She had three days to change his mind.

Chapter Eight

THE VERY FIRST step in changing a man's mind, Laurel discovered during the remainder of the week, was having access to it. And that, Sawyer cleverly managed to deny her.

She awoke early Saturday morning in the sunny yellow bedroom that was hers whenever she visited Jasper's stately Virginia home, stricken with a dull headache and a pounding sense of frustration. She didn't like being thwarted, especially when the stakes were so high. Of course, she'd expected the challenge of persuading Sawyer to back off to be roughly equal to that of rowing a leaky canoe up a waterfall. When she hadn't expected was to be outwitted before she even climbed into the damn boat.

The most obvious ploy to see him had met with immediate failure. Her services as tour guide were no longer required. Nor, obviously, was her presence in any way, shape, or form. Actually, no longer *desired* would be a more apt description. Sawyer made that fact very clear by simply being unavailable. Her phone calls went unreturned, her borderline frantic notes requesting a meeting with him were ignored, save for one curt reply stating that he would see her at Jasper's on Friday.

It was obvious that he had set this weekend as the deadline for dropping his bombshell about her past, and yet Laurel found herself hanging back from the inevitable task of confessing everything to Jasper. Most likely it was simply cowardice that kept her silent, but she also couldn't shake the feeling that something was out of focus about the way she was seeing this whole situation.

It had to do with the way Sawyer had looked at her the night of the British reception, in those last few seconds before Jasper had interrupted them. The thrill of victory hadn't burned in his eyes as he'd stared at her. Neither had bitterness or disgust or any of the other emotions she'd expected, and what had been there instead haunted her more than anything else could have. It had been sadness—the stunned, bone-chilling kind of sadness that prevents you from saying or doing anything—that she had glimpsed in that unguarded sliver of time before he once more retreated behind a wall of icy control.

Laurel struggled to understand what that might mean and kept coming back to the possibility that she'd been wrong in her accusations. Unfortunately, both the facts as reported by an increasingly impatient Bill Reynolds and the unyielding common sense that ruled her life contradicted that. So, as often as it cropped up, she dismissed the notion of Sawyer's innocence as wishful thinking.

Still, it was hard not to wish. If only she were wrong about Sawyer's intentions . . . certainly it would be a blessing for poor, unsuspecting Jasper. And her own untidy secret would be safe for a while longer. Although amazingly, that was no longer Laurel's number one concern. She was much more preoccupied with feelings of guilt over the way her mistakes were threatening Jasper's future. Along with another, much more selfish reason for wishing she was wrong about Sawyer.

If she were, then what had happened between them the night they'd spent together would not have been the humiliating lie she now knew it to be. Instead it would have been the sweet, long awaited miracle it had seemed at the time. And then maybe, just maybe, all the dreams she'd spun during that long, sleepless adventure in his arms might have a chance to come true.

Of course, all that was wishful thinking carried to its most absurd degree. Even if Sawyer weren't hell-bent on destroying her, Laurel knew there was another obstacle standing gracefully in the way of their sharing anything more meaningful than bad memories. She was reminded of it several hundred times a day when her feelings of guilt and dread were suddenly interrupted by unexpected, wretchedly vivid images of Sawyer and Maureen whiling away these warm perfect days with which Mother Nature had perversely seen fit to bless their visit to Washington. She was quickly coming to hate the very sight of cherry blossoms and cheerful street vendors and all the other romantic signs of spring.

Last night had done little to dissuade Laurel from her suspicion that Sawyer and Maureen might share more than business interests. Jasper had gotten the weekend off to a congenial start with an elegant dinner party, and Sawyer and Maureen had spent all five courses, as well as cocktails and brandy, by each other's side. True, their behavior wasn't exactly fawning—scrutinize as she might, Laurel could detect nothing in their treatment of each other that suggested they were more than friends. And she supposed it was natural for them to stick together, seeing as neither of them knew any of the other weekend guests who included several of Jasper's close advisers along with his daughter and son-in-law.

That is, neither of them knew anyone except her, of whom Sawyer had distressingly intimate knowledge. The unbidden recollection of just how intimate—and varied—sent Laurel shooting out of bed and into the private bath adjoining her room with flaming cheeks and recharged determination.

She showered and dressed quickly, purposely selecting a bright yellow cotton sundress sashed with crimson that lifted her spirits, making her feel bold and unstoppable. Sawyer might have been successful with his little safety-in-numbers game of cat and mouse last evening, but this was a new day. And Maureen better be prepared to spend a few minutes of it alone. One way or another she was going to corner Sawyer privately and make a final, last-ditch effort to halt the quickly descending ax of disaster.

To reach the dining room, she had to trek down the wide curving stairs, past the fountain in the center hall, and through a formal parlor larger than most one-family homes. The only other living soul she encountered along the way was wearing a white ruffled apron over a black maid's uniform.

The maid nodded at Laurel with a cheerful smile as she deposited a crystal cylinder of yellow tulips on the dining-room table. "Good morning, Ms. Forrest."

"Good morning, Sandy," Laurel returned, recognizing the young woman from her previous visits. "Am I the first one up today?"

"Oh, no. Mr. Dane's already had breakfast. He and Mr. Lewiston are in the study. They did ask not to be disturbed, though," she added with a politely apologetic air.

The last thing in the world Laurel wanted was to disturb Jasper, especially with news that was bound to send his private world spinning off its axis.

"That's fine," she said. "I think I'll just take my coffee and sit outside on the terrace."

The housemaid nodded. "It looks like it's going to be a beautiful day."

Time would tell about that, thought Laurel. Trying to quell an anxiety pang over what lay ahead, she reached for one of the delicate china cups arranged on the long sideboard. Next to them sat a sterling silver coffee urn as well as several trays of breakfast pastries and croissants. The chef, she knew, was already on duty in the kitchen, prepared to whip up omelettes or waffles or whatever else Jasper's guests fancied for breakfast. Settling for a cup of black coffee and a plain croissant, she carried them outside to the patio overlooking the pool and made herself as comfortable as the state of her nerves permitted at one of several round umbrella-topped tables.

So, it appeared society not only arrived late, as the old saying went, they also arose late. Which didn't account for Sawyer's absence, she mused wryly. The fact that his folks had eked out a living running a small store while hers had been drifting ne'er-do-wells before settling in Beaumont only brought him an insignificant half-step closer to being manor-born than she was.

And besides, Sawyer had always been a morning person. Although she had denied it to him the other day, the fact was she remembered well driving down to the beach together so early in the morning that the world looked all soft and pink around the edges. Her world, anyway—which may well have had more to do with Sawyer's presence in it than with the time of day. He had always been wide awake and full of enthusiasm those mornings. Eager. Energetic. She smiled, remembering. Untirable, really. The heat of the vivid memory slowly melted through Laurel, starting that old, twisting feeling in the pit of her stomach.

She nearly jumped off her seat when the door behind her slid open. Jerking her head around, she found

Maureen hesitating with one foot still inside and the other out.

"Oh, Laurel," she said, looking a little surprised to find her up so early. "Good morning. Do you mind if I join you?"

"Of course not," Laurel lied, executing a bright smile and a gracious sweep of her hand to indicate the other empty chairs at her table.

Maureen's responding smile was tinged with relief, suggesting that she was as wary of Laurel as Laurel was of her. She crossed the patio slowly, carefully balancing a full cup of coffee and a plate that held a cherry cheese danish and a pecan roll.

"I couldn't decide which of these I wanted," she explained a bit sheepishly. As she lowered the crowded plate to the table, she shot it a look that was part contempt, part anticipation. "And I couldn't resist either." She sat down, and as her fanny hit the chair cushion her eyes became wide circles of shocked blue. "But, oh God, I should have," she nearly wailed.

"Should have what?" demanded Laurel, alarmed by her expression and her tone.

"Resisted," Maureen countered, settling into a slightly more composed look of disgust. She appeared to be waging an internal war of wills for a few seconds, then with a shrug she leaned across the table and in a quiet, conspiratorial tone said, "My pants . . . the back seam just turned into the Great Divide. And it's all Sawyer's fault . . . damn him."

Laurel had no idea what to say. She desperately wanted to know—but wasn't sure she actually wanted to have to sit there and hear—what Sawyer had to do with this woman's pants.

"Where is Sawyer?" she finally asked in a ridiculously offhand way.

Maureen was too preoccupied to notice Laurel's total lack of reaction to her crisis. Her teeth clamped anxiously over her bottom lip as she apparently tried to assess the damage with her fingers.

"Who knows?" she grumbled. "Is there a car dealer nearby?"

"I beg your pardon?"

"A car dealer," she repeated. "The man's obsessed. Ever since I got there, he's been dragging me around to every car dealership within a hundred-mile radius... make that two hundred miles. After the first two or three, I started waiting in the car. Then I started noticing all these cute little refreshment carts that seem to be parked on every corner around here. When I'm bored, I eat," she admitted with a rueful shrug. "I've eaten enough frozen yogurt and pretzels in the past three days to pay for a damn car. And now I'm getting my just desserts... no pun intended. You know," she continued, "I should have realized these slacks were the wrong choice when I had to lie down on the bed to get them zipped."

Maureen's expression was so forlorn that Laurel couldn't help feeling sympathy for her plight. Which was probably a little traitorous, she thought, remembering what happened to houses divided against themselves. She was accustomed to looking beyond the surface with people she met, even while keeping tight wraps on her own secret self, but even she couldn't detect anything coy or devious about the other woman's manner. And if Maureen did have some ulterior motive for seeking Laurel out, she certainly could have found a less embarrassing way to strike up a conversation than splitting her pants in public.

Luckily, watching her weight was not a concern for Laurel, but if it were, and if she'd been sitting on the other side of this table, she would have kept her mouth shut and found some way to slink away before her problem was detected. Certainly she would never have confided to a virtual stranger about it with the casual resignation Maureen had just displayed. The fact that she was confident enough to do such a thing struck a cord of admiration in Laurel. In spite of herself, she liked the woman. And she wished she could respond to the situation with the sort of consoling, lighthearted remark she knew it called for, the sort that would come easily to most women's lips. But that spirit of feminine camaraderie, which should have been her birthright, was beyond Laurel . . . and always had been.

She'd never had a best friend or even, for that matter, a particularly close friend . . . except, of course, for Sawyer. The embarrassment of not ever being able to reciprocate a girlfriend's invitations or, worse, of having someone show up unexpectedly and witness one of her father's binges wasn't worth the risk. Later, after striking out on her own, it wasn't fear of embarrassment that made her keep everyone—male and female acquaintances alike—at an emotional distance. It was fear of exposure.

So here she was, twenty-nine years old, a successful professional who regularly rubbed elbows with dignitaries from all over the world, fumbling for the appropriate response to another woman's honest vulnerability.

While Laurel stalled by sipping her coffee in silence, Maureen had been contemplating the plate before her with mounting interest. With a sigh of surrender, she finally picked up the cherry-topped danish and took a bite.

"What the heck? The damage has already been done now," she rationalized flippantly. Pushing the plate with the pecan roll toward Laurel, she added, "But whatever it takes, stop me from eating that one, too."

Laurel laughed, then impulsively lifted the napkin from her lap and draped it over the roll.

"Great idea!" Maureen declared. "Out of sight, out of mind . . . do you think it will work?"

"That probably depends on how hungry you are," countered Laurel.

"That's just it." With another long sigh, Maureen banished the partially nibbled danish to a spot under the napkin as well and plopped her chin in her hand. "I'm not really hungry." Her lips quirked into a self-effacing smile. "Unfortunately, I also eat whenever I'm on edge. Believe me, Sawyer Gates is going to owe me an entire new wardrobe by the time we get home."

Laurel's curiosity surged, but she calmly hid it behind another sip of coffee. "You and Sawyer seem very . . . close," she remarked, as if making the most casual of observations.

"Yeah, too close, I sometimes think. If we weren't, if things were strictly business between us, maybe I'd be more in control."

Her eyes narrowed as she evidently discerned the wave of disappointment Laurel was valiantly trying to hide. "Oh dear, you meant *close* close," she exclaimed, her enlightened nod quickly giving way to a quizzical lowering of tawny eyebrows. "Is that what you were getting at earlier, when you asked me where Sawyer was? Were you really asking if I had firsthand knowledge about whether or not he was still in bed?"

The bull's-eye observation made Laurel shift uneasily in her chair. "Of course not. I just . . . you were . . ."

"You're the woman." It was a statement, not a question, breathed in a quiet, almost awestruck tone. With it, a mysterious look of understanding settled on Maureen's face.

"The woman?" Laurel echoed, afraid of just how intuitive Maureen might prove to be.

She nodded slowly. "Right. He never talks about it, of course, but I've always known without actually knowing, if you know what I mean, that there was a woman—one important woman—in Sawyer's past. There usually is when a guy's as hard a case as he is."

Eyes glittering, she regarded Laurel with fresh interest. "Now it all makes sense. Sawyer's mood, his sudden change of mind . . ." She trailed off, as if she was
simply cataloging for her own benefit each piece of the
puzzle that fell into place. "Maybe that's why you
seemed so familiar. Right from the start I had this feeling I knew you from somewhere."

Laurel's heart jammed into her throat and thudded to
a halt, only resuming its jackhammer pounding when
Maureen shrugged and continued.

"But I guess it's just that I know Sawyer so well—I
mean strictly as a friend, of course," she amended hastily, "that I was picking up on his signals or the vibrations between you two or something. I can't believe I
didn't figure it out sooner, though . . . like the other
night when the two of you were going at it in the hallway. A professional difference of opinion, Sawyer told
me." She made a scoffing sound. "And I fell for it."

A part of Laurel felt like dancing around the table
and hugging Maureen because she was Sawyer's friend
and not his lover. Another more practical part of her
managed a small laugh and an incredulous shake of her
head. All of her was praying that Maureen would fall
for her line as easily as she had Sawyer's.

"Maureen, I don't know what Sawyer told you or
what you *think* you've figured out," she said, "but I'm
afraid I have to disappoint you. I am not some mystery
woman from Sawyer Gates's past."

The nervous cadence of her voice was obvious even
to Laurel, and she wasn't the least bit surprised when
Maureen stared at her with open skepticism.

"Really? That's a shame, because I've always had
this feeling that Sawyer needed to meet up with that
woman again—if only to exorcise some private demon
that drives him to prove himself." Leaning forward on
both elbows, she quickly added, "I mean, don't get me
wrong, I can understand wanting to be successful and

rich . . . oh boy, do I ever understand it! But the money's not the thing for Sawyer. Neither is the power nor the recognition it brings. It's as if he needs something more, something personal, to validate his success. I think he needs to see everything he's sweated to achieve reflected in that woman's eyes before it really counts."

Laurel's mouth opened, then closed, and she licked her suddenly dry lips before producing a very wavery, "That's crazy. How could someone he knew so long ago matter so much?"

"I never said how long ago it was," Maureen pointed out. "I really have no idea about that . . . except that it was before I got to know him."

Laurel's flush deepened. "It's still crazy."

"Well, so's life. Haven't you ever noticed?"

"I'm not the woman you're talking about," Laurel insisted softly.

"Then I'm sorry I even brought it up." She paused before asking, "But if you were that woman, would it be so hard to cut Sawyer a break after all this time?"

Maureen's question made it clear that she didn't give much credence to Laurel's denial. But she didn't pressure her for an answer, not with her tone or with her expression, which was as unruffled and unthreatening as a warm bath. If she had, Laurel might have been able to gather her defenses and dismiss the matter with an icy glare.

Instead, she felt an unfamiliar longing rise up inside her, a yearning to share with someone the questions and worries she'd been shouldering all alone for days now. Cut Sawyer a break? Did Maureen have any idea of what the man was planning to do to her? Some inner sense told Laurel that she didn't, in spite of the business ties they shared, or she wouldn't be sitting here talking as freely as she was. Whereas only an hour ago she'd viewed Maureen as a one-dimensional "other woman," their conversation this morning had dispelled that notion. Maureen's attempt to be friendly was honest, and she would be just as honest—and compassionate—a listener, Laurel felt certain. If ony Laurel knew what to say.

Her life ever since she'd left Beaumont had been a race, a race to get somewhere and be someone, and a race to get as far away as she could from what she used to be. With a sudden clear view into the future, Laurel realized that the finish line—if there even was one for such a race—wasn't yet in sight. And she was tired of running, tired of hiding, tired of never having a friend or being one.

She had always feared it would be hard to stop running, but it wasn't. The decision was made without fanfare, and certainly with less forethought than she habitually applied to much less important matters. And it felt wonderful. Immediately, instead of a frenzied blur that had to be constantly analyzed, Laurel saw her future—at least, her immediate future—in clear sequence. For once there were no contingency plans or alternate strategies complicating the path ahead. She knew exactly what had to be done.

The next second the door behind her slid open again, and Sawyer ambled onto the patio. In spite of what he'd put her through this week—would *still* be putting her through if she hadn't just awoken from this self-imposed bad dream her life had turned into—Laurel felt a tremor that was like a small earthquake in her soul at the sight of him. He was wearing an old pair of Levi's that molded the lean lines of his hips and thighs with well-worn intimacy. A white cotton shirt, open at the neck, contrasted dramatically with the polished bronze of his skin.

"Good morning," he drawled, sweeping both women with his smile, but his eyes touched Laurel first and clung.

Before she could swallow the cotton in her mouth to respond, Maureen was out of her seat.

"Morning, Sawyer, remind me to talk to you about a new wardrobe. For now, though, stay right where you are," she ordered in a rush. To Laurel, she added, "I'm going to make my escape before the audience grows any larger."

Laurel couldn't help laughing as she watched Maureen inch her way to the door, careful to face a bewildered, amused Sawyer at all times.

"Maureen," she called a second before the door shut. "I just remembered I have a sewing kit in with my makeup. It's on the dresser in my room—first one on the left at the top of the stairs. Help yourself."

Maureen smiled. "Thanks, Laurel. Maybe someday I can return the favor."

You already have, thought Laurel. Hopefully, someday she would even have a chance to tell Maureen that. But first there were other things that had to be taken care of, and things that had to be said. Not to Sawyer, she realized now, but to Jasper.

"What's her problem?" inquired Sawyer, inclining his head in the direction Maureen had just disappeared.

"It's . . . I think I'd better let her explain that later," Laurel decided to say. Getting to her feet as Sawyer dropped into the chair across from her, she murmured, "You'll have to excuse me. There's something I have to take care of."

Surprise flickered in Sawyer's eyes. "Is this the same woman who all week has been so hot to talk with me . . . *privately?*" he added in an exaggerated drawl that called to Laurel's mind the way she had underlined that same word in her note to him.

"As a matter of fact," she said on impulse, "it's not. This is an entirely new woman."

Sawyer's brows lifted. "Another one?" he inquired dryly.

Was she strong enough to shove him, chair and all, backward into the pool? Probably not, she concluded ruefully and settled for a smug, pitying shake of her head as she turned to go.

"You really aren't going to stay and talk to me?" Sawyer demanded, amazement deep in his voice. "You don't want one last chance to plead Dane's case?"

Slowly, Laurel swung back to face him. Not even his taunts could chase the sparkle from her mood this morning. "No, I don't."

His lips curved in a small sardonic smile. "Why not, Laurel? Did you manage to come up with some way to let him go down the tubes without dragging you with him?"

She was wrong. Sparkle wasn't very sturdy stuff, after all. Covering the distance between them in a heartbeat, she stood glaring down at him. "You're really enjoying this, aren't you? You didn't grant me these few days of grace out of the goodness of your heart . . . you did it because you wanted me to squirm a while longer."

"If you're asking if I enjoy seeing you suspended over a fire you yourself started and kept fueled, just waiting for you to drop, I guess the answer is yes."

The words lashed around her like whips. She hadn't even dared formulate the thought, but deep down she'd been fool enough to hope that the fresh start she was resolved to make might extend to her relationship with Sawyer as well. If they'd been able to move past the mistakes and the bitterness, they might have at least been able to salvage a friendship out of all they'd once shared.

Surveying the muscles of his face and arms, all rigid with suppressed emotion, she realized that was about as likely as having time move backward.

"You must really hate me," she whispered, the ache that tore through her as powerful as a physical blow.

"Hate you?" Sawyer's eyes narrowed to slits, hiding

whatever he was feeling behind a shield of black velvet lashes. Without warning, his hand shot out to grab her wrist and with one sharp jerk she was in his lap.

"Hate you, you little fool? Oh, I won't say I didn't try to hate you," he growled, easily quelling her best efforts to wrench free. "But it didn't work. I guess I'm not quite as efficient at mastering my destiny as you are with yours." Wrapping his hand in her hair, he pulled hard until her face tipped up to his.

"Hate you?" he repeated again, as if stunned by the very idea. "My God, woman, I love you."

Watching his mouth descend, Laurel fully expected her own was about to be ravaged. Instead, he took her with such tenderness it left her reeling. With his tongue, he nudged her lips apart, and she was helpless to stop him. He flicked across the soft sides of her mouth, tasting, exploring, savoring. A hum of anticipation started in her breasts and rippled downward.

She didn't actively participate—she wasn't that dazed—but she didn't actively resist either. And when his hand cupped her hip, pulling her tightly against the tumescence below his belt, and his tongue took up the slow thrusting rhythm evocative of a much more intimate union, her soft whimper wasn't one of protest.

A honeyed warmth was spreading through her, making her soft and pliable, heating her until she feared she really might melt right out of his arms and end up in a puddle at his feet.

And then she suddenly saw with reluctant clarity, Sawyer's victory would be complete. He would have taken her, thrown it in her face, then proved that with the snap of his fingers and a husky declaration of love, he could do it all over again. She really was a fool. He could say he loved her a million times, he could write it across the sky in twenty-four-carat gold letters and that wouldn't make it true.

"No." She jerked her mouth away from his and, catching him off guard, managed to struggle to her feet. "I don't believe you." The words poured from her with an anguished sob. "I'll never believe you again."

"I wasn't aware you ever had," Sawyer said coldly.

Only vaguely did Laurel register that the look on his face didn't back up his contemptuous tone. His eyes were shadowed and his mouth twisted in that injured-looking grimace. She was too fortified with inner rage to care. Her thoughts were black and bitter as she rushed toward the door.

It took every ounce of willpower Sawyer possessed not to go after her. Only the fear of what he might do when he got his hands on her kept him riveted to his seat. Never believe him again, huh? Well, he'd see about that. Although it was obviously going to take longer than he'd first thought.

It had once been his foolish hope that if he scraped away all the layers of facade, on the most basic, gut level, Laurel trusted him. Their hurried conversation outside the British reception the other night had effectively squelched that fantasy. Her unquestioning acceptance of the idea that he could make love to her with the soul-searing completeness that he had, and then use her, sell her out, to get at Jasper—or worse, just for the vengeful pleasure of seeing her destroyed—had enraged him to a point closer to violence than he'd been since that long-ago night when she'd walked out on him.

Once the pain and crushing anger had worked through his system, however, he had stoically accepted the fact that it wasn't that Laurel didn't trust *him;* she didn't trust anyone. And with good reason, he supposed, living on quicksand the way she had for the past eleven years. Somehow Laurel had forgotten what it meant to have complete and utter faith in another human being. If she'd ever really understood it in the first place.

Well, all that was going to change. If children and animals could be taught to trust, so, by God, could she. And Sawyer was determined he'd either be the one to teach her or he'd go to his grave trying.

Chapter Nine

JASPER'S STUDY WAS situated in the opposite wing of the house from the dining and living rooms. That side of the house, always quiet, sounded even more so to Laurel this morning. The hallway leading to the study seemed a thousand miles long, and its beautifully carved oak door looked as intimidating to her as the gates of hell.

Twice she approached it and changed her mind, retreating to her room for a while to rationalize that she simply didn't want to disturb the men in conference. Finally, on the third try, convinced that the anticipation had to be every bit as excruciating as the deed itself, she marshaled the courage to knock.

Jasper accepted her interruption with good grace and only mild surprise. Ted Lewiston quickly excused himself to get a cup of coffee, and then she and Jasper were alone, sitting on opposite sides of his wide desk.

"All right, Laurel," he said. "What is this urgent matter we have to discuss?"

"It's not exactly something we have to discuss," she explained, contradicting what she'd said only a moment ago. "It's more something I have to tell you . . . I guess you might call it a confession."

Jasper was a man accustomed to schooling his thoughts, so it was no surprise to Laurel that he met that announcement with nothing more alarmed than a slight nod.

"Go on," he invited.

"Bill Reynolds came to me earlier this week," she began in the hope that their conversation might be an easy starting point for telling him the whole messy truth. "He was concerned that you . . . actually, I was concerned . . ."

She was wrong; there was no easy way to begin this. With a sigh, she confessed, "The truth is that I've been keeping the truth from you for a long time."

Jasper smiled gently. "Laurel, if it makes you feel any better, Bill called me himself yesterday, after he decided you were dragging your heels on this thing. And, in fact, I had already heard rumors about what Riordon and young Gates were planning as early as Wednesday morning. I appreciate your efforts to protect me the way you did—although I have to admit I can't for the life of me understand why you thought it necessary."

"I was . . . only trying to help," Laurel interjected weakly.

"Yes, well, I've handled crises in my career before, my dear, and I'm sure I will again. The important thing," he continued with an emphatic pound on the desk, "is to nip these things in the bud. As it stands now, I find myself with my back to the wall and little time to maneuver. That's the reason Ted and I have been closeted in here most of the morning, trying to decide on an appropriate course of action."

"I realize that," Laurel told him. "That's why it was so important that I talk with you right away, before you reach any decision about what you should do."

"I'm afraid there is only one thing I can do, Laurel," Jasper responded. He sat with his shoulders resting easily against the back of the chair; his fingers folded, not clenched, in front of him. It was the posture of a man used to making hard decisions and sticking with them no matter what. "I didn't choose the game, but I still have to play it, even if Gates does seem to be holding all the best cards. I have too much at stake—and too much pride—not to call."

Laurel sprang forward in her seat. "For pity's sake, Jasper, this isn't a poker game, it's your life, everything you've dreamed of. You can't just call Sawyer's bluff and hope for the best. He means what he says, Jasper, believe me. He's not the sort of man to back down from a fight."

"There'll be no fight," Jasper countered with quiet conviction. "I believe in this country, Laurel, and I believe in the system that makes it great. I'm prepared to go into that Senate confirmation hearing, make a full disclosure, and have them turn their brightest spotlight on my past. I'm willing to own up to my mistakes and stand on my own record. Because I believe that, in the end, that will be all that really counts."

Laurel was paralyzed with guilt. If at that instant the earth had opened up and swallowed her and never spit her back, she wouldn't have complained. Anything was preferable to being the one responsible for extinguishing that glow of pride and determination in Jasper's eyes.

She prayed that he was right, that ultimately those evaluating his worthiness to serve as ambassador would consider his own many accomplishments to be of greater importance than his unfortunate, brief personal association with her. But whether that proved to be true or not, he deserved to know up front exactly how the cards were stacked against him.

"Jasper, I admire your courage, I really do. And I wish for your sake that things were that simple. Unfortunately, there are ... complications."

He pressed his fingertips together and frowned at her over the top of them. "Such as?"

"Me," she shot back, the contempt in her tone entirely self-directed. "I'm the complication that just might destroy you."

"I think you'd better explain," he suggested.

Taking a deep breath, Laurel plunged in. She had hoped the telling might be easier this second time, but instead it was worse. With Sawyer, there had been an unspoken sense of acceptance even before she opened up to him. Looking back now, she realized, it must have been all in her head, but at least when she'd made that terrifying virgin leap into truth, she'd believed he was ready and willing to cushion her fall.

Telling Jasper was closer to working the high wire without a net. He might react with understanding or with cold fury. His expression, as she forced out each shameful detail of her past, gave no hint of what he was thinking, and she had no way of gauging his feelings. With Jasper, there was no trace of that feeling of being linked on a deeper, almost spiritual level that she had once shared with Sawyer. It occurred to Laurel, as she struggled to string the facts together in a sensible order, that in a very real way telling Jasper was like telling a stranger. The fact that she'd ever thought she could marry and spend the rest of her life with him was only proof of the extent of her self-delusion.

By the time she finished, there were tears streaking her cheeks; tears for Jasper and for herself, for dreams broken and time wasted. She felt sad and frustrated, as well as a bit apprehensive, knowing she may still have to face the very righteous explosion of his anger.

No matter. Buoying her through that tempest of emotions and doubts was a sense of peace. Unlike the sort of contentment she'd experienced up until then, those fleeting spells between the realization of one goal and the race for the next, Laurel knew this time the peace was hers to keep. She had paid too heavy a price to squander it or endanger it ever again.

"So," Jasper said quietly when she fell silent, "you're neither who you say you are, nor what you say you are. Is there anything else I should know?"

"Yes. I want you to know that I'm sorry I involved you in this. If I had known how it would end up . . . if I'd had any idea . . ." She dropped her gaze to where her hands twisted nervously in her lap. "I'm just so sorry."

"And you're also shaking," observed Jasper. "With guilt, I imagine. Misplaced guilt, I should add."

His gentle concern only made it worse. She wished he would yell at her, pound the desk, throw something. Anything except talk to her in that calm, soothing voice. She didn't deserve to be soothed.

"Don't, Jasper," she protested. "Don't try to tell me that this doesn't matter."

"I wouldn't dream of trying to tell you anything so stupid. Of course it matters. Your past matters very much . . . but primarily to you. And that's as it should be."

"Don't you understand? It's not *me* I'm worried about, Jasper."

"Good, then you can stop shaking . . . because it's not your background—as shameful as I'm sure it seems to you at this moment—that threatens my confirmation. It's my own."

Laurel jerked her head up to look at him with a bewildered frown. "I don't understand."

"Of course not. You see, I've been as . . . selective in

telling you about myself as you've been with me. It's not unusual to want to keep one's dirty linen hidden, Laurel. Especially from someone you're trying to impress," he added, his mouth touched with amusement. "I think we've both been guilty of that."

"Maybe. But I did more than hide some dirty linen. What I did was tantamount to lying." She groaned, burying her face in her hands. "There I go again, whitewashing the facts. What I did *was* lying, period."

"What you did was make a mistake. We all make them. Yours was worse than some, but not nearly as bad as a great deal of others." He stood, coming around to lean against the corner of the desk nearest her.

Still unable to return his reassuring smile, Laurel at least managed to drop her hands and face him. "I can't imagine anything much worse," she muttered.

"Then you don't have much of an imagination . . . but judging from the story you just told me, I don't think that's the case at all." He paused and for a moment the only sound in the room was the ticking of the grandfather clock in the corner.

"Laurel," he said finally, "I appreciate your honesty in telling me what you did. I know it was a very difficult thing to do, but you did it because you thought it would help me. Now I'd like to return the favor."

Laurel's tawny lashes fluttered in bewilderment. "I'm not sure I understand."

"I'd like to tell you something about my past, something that I've told very, very few people over the years. It's as hard for me to talk about as what you just told me is for you."

"Jasper, there's no need . . ."

He halted her protest with a raised hand. "Please, let me speak. When I was a young man," he began quickly, as if not wanting time to change his mind, "my father had ties—very strong ties, I'm afraid—to organized crime. He was the man in charge of the local numbers racket, a very lucrative business in the Chicago neighborhood where I grew up. I knew it was wrong, and I knew it was illegal, but I got involved anyway. I thought then that it was the quickest way to get ahead, to be somebody important. It was a youthful mistake . . . not unlike your own."

His revelations came as a shock to Laurel. She'd known he was a self-made man, but little more. Like so many other subjects, the details of their respective pasts were something they had never discussed. Jasper didn't comment on her stunned expression . . . if he even noticed. It seemed to Laurel that he was looking at her and through her at the same time. Peering into his past, she suspected, much the way she had been taking a closer look at her own lately.

"I wasn't in the *business* very long," he continued, "when I realized that wasn't the way I wanted to live. Having to be always on the lookout, always afraid you'd slip up or that someone would sell you out to save his own skin. It's not an easy life."

"I know," Laurel said softly.

Jasper leaned forward to pat her hand, his look tender. "Yes, in a way I imagine you do know. At any rate, I soon come to the sad conclusion that the only shortcut to wealth and success is being born to it. And I certainly hadn't been . . . anymore than you were, Laurel. It was very hard for me to tell my father I wanted out of his operation, but one day I got up the nerve to do it. I moved away, got a job in the mailroom of a small newspaper, and began the long, hard climb to where I am today." He glanced around the spacious, expensively decorated study. "Not bad for a kid from the wrong side of nowhere, hmm?"

Laurel didn't overlook the sorrow behind his smile. "Not bad at all," she concurred with the same gentleness he'd shown her earlier.

"For a long time after that, I didn't see my father or

anyone else in my family. I became Jasper Dane, an important man, not Jasper Danilkowski, a punk whose father paid the bills by collecting ten-cent bets from old ladies. I was ashamed of him, you see, and I was afraid that if anyone found out what sort of stock I came from, I would be right back where I started. Then one day I woke up and realized that I missed my family much more than I was ashamed of them."

"Did you call them? See them?" Laurel demanded anxiously as he paused.

Jasper nodded, then crossed the room to stare out the floor-to-ceiling window overlooking the tennis courts. "By then, though, my father had passed away. I made a vow the first time I visited his grave that whenever the subject came up, I would never again deny who I was or where I came from." He swung back to face Laurel. "From that day to this, I never have. I won't start now."

"I admire your conviction, Jasper," Laurel told him truthfully.

"I wasn't looking for praise, Laurel. I told you all this for two reasons. First, so that you'll leave this room with a clear conscience, knowing that nothing you've said or done will affect the outcome of that hearing."

Laurel's jaw dropped. She'd been so caught up in Jasper's heart-wrenching story, she hadn't thought about how it affected her personally. "Are you sure? They may be planning to air both our dirty linen . . ."

Jasper cut her off with a definitive shake of his head. "I've looked into the matter and I know for a fact that what I've just told you is the background information in question."

"If that's true," she breathed with amazement, "then I was wrong about Sawyer . . . he wasn't going to betray me."

Her heart soared, then nose-dived like a glider caught in a downwind. With wrenching clarity, she recalled all her angry, bitter accusations. If Sawyer hadn't betrayed her trust, hadn't simply been using her all along, what possible motive could he have for making love to her? For soothing her fears? For saying he loved her? Something sharp and jagged seemed to be slicing across her heart. And what, she wondered frantically, did it say about her that she was so willing to believe the very worst about him?

Jasper, witnessing the telltale parade of emotions streaking across her face, lifted his heavy gray brows in a silent question.

"You see," Laurel began in a hurried attempt to explain the fervor of her last remark, "somehow that day you asked me to show him around town, we talked and I ended up telling Sawyer the truth about me."

Jasper nodded without commenting.

Knowing what he was no doubt realizing as he put two and two together, Laurel blushed and shifted restlessly. "Actually, Jasper, when I told you the story of my life a few minutes ago, I left out one small detail ...I did know Sawyer Gates back in Beaumont. We sort of went together in high school."

What a ridiculously inadequate explanation, Laurel thought, without having the slightest idea how to better capture in words all that she and Sawyer had once been to each other.

"We recognized each other right away, of course," she went on, "but he played along with the ruse for my sake. Then when Bill told me that Sawyer had discovered some background information to use against you, I naturally assumed it was what I had told him about myself the night before." She shook her head in remorse. "I figured he was going to punish you and get his revenge at the same time."

"Revenge?" echoed Jasper, frown lines puckering his brow. "Are you sure Sawyer Gates was only a small detail in your life?"

The flames in Laurel's cheeks flared higher. "More like a massive detail," she admitted.

"I half-suspected as much," Jasper shocked her by revealing. "There's something in the air whenever you two are within gazing distance that makes a romantic old man wonder."

Laurel shot to her feet, approaching him with an apprehensive step. "Jasper, I'm so sorry . . . that's another reason I had to talk with you. I know there's nothing official between you and me, but . . . but even if this thing with my past hadn't come up, I couldn't go on seeing you."

"May I ask why?"

Laurel sighed. She'd learned late, but she *had* learned that you don't pledge to love, honor, and cherish a man you don't. And if you are lucky enough to find a man you do feel all that for, you don't leave him behind to go chasing shadows. "Because we don't love each other," she said regretfully.

"My dear, whoever said we did?" With a wide smile, Jasper let her slip gracefully off the hook. "And are you in love with Gates?"

"I'm not sure," she replied softly. Soon, now, she was going to have to reach deep inside for an honest answer to that question she'd been avoiding asking herself.

"But, maybe?"

"Maybe," she admitted.

"Then my second reason for telling you about my own past is even more important." He moved closer and took both her hands in his. "The past exists, Laurel. It can't be wiped clean no matter how hard we try or how far we run. The trick is to come to terms with it. Because until you do, you'll never truly be happy . . . and you'll never make anyone else happy, either. And that, Laurel, is what I wish for you . . . true happiness."

For the second time, tears clouded Laurel's vision. "That sounds like a good-bye speech."

Giving her hands a squeeze, Jasper asked, "Shouldn't it?"

She nodded. "I suppose so. But I'd be glad to stick by you through the hearings ... unless you think that will hurt your chances?"

"If you're going to do what I surmise you plan to— take steps to clear up the discrepancies in your past— then I would have to say your presence at the hearings ... wouldn't help," he finished tactfully. Grinning, he added, "Besides, I imagine you'll be kept quite busy straightening out matters of your own. If we're lucky, maybe we can manage to avoid the fallout from each other's bombshell."

"Then, here's to luck." Smiling back at him, Laurel stretched on tiptoe to kiss his cheek. "Good-bye, Jasper. And thanks."

Just as she reached the door he called to her.

"Laurel, one more thing ... for what it's worth. While they were digging, my sources didn't turn up any mention of you at all. I'd say your secret never went any further than Gates." He reached for his glasses, his attention already straying to the open folder he'd pushed aside when she first walked in. "And please ask Ted to get back in here, will you?"

Ted was already waiting right outside, and, as Laurel finished closing the door behind him, she smiled. No need to worry that she may have broken poor Jasper's heart. The nonchalant way he'd accepted the end of their relationship was bad for her pride, but great for her morale ... and right now that needed all the boosts it could get. His parting shot about Sawyer hadn't been quite as uplifting.

Of course, Jasper must have put his wide-ranging newsmen's sources to work delving into the threat Sawyer and Mike Riordon presented from the first moment he'd learned of the seriousness of their opposition to him. If he said Sawyer hadn't revealed to anyone else what she'd confided in him, Laurel believed it. It was the final absolution of Sawyer's sins . . . correction, the sins she'd invented and found him guilty of without bothering to ask for a word of explanation.

Unbidden, the memory of his face and the ache in his voice the other night when he'd turned her question around and asked, "How could *you?*" flashed into Laurel's mind and refused to be willed away. It was a haunting vision, as effective as any chain ever used for self-flagellation, and so vivid, she was almost at the end of the long hall before she noticed Sawyer up ahead, standing beside the fountain.

He was alone, and she didn't have to think twice to deduce why he'd chosen to linger where he had. To get to anyplace in the house, you had to pass through this center hall. It was exactly the right spot to wait for someone, and Laurel knew exactly for whom Sawyer was waiting.

The problem was, she wasn't ready to face him. Not yet. She had no idea what to say, how to begin to undo the damage she'd done. She needed time, and she had a hunch Sawyer would not be in a patient mood. He would no doubt be more furious with her than ever after this morning's little scene. What really twisted the knife was that he had every right to be.

She had been so sure he'd broken his word to her, just the way he seemed to have broken it years ago. Instead, it was she who had repeated a past mistake. She hadn't trusted Sawyer enough to wait back then, and she hadn't trusted him enough this time to give him the benefit of the doubt.

Sawyer had been standing with his back to her. When he made a move to turn, Laurel's panic exploded like an overinflated balloon. Whirling around, she started back down the hallway, impulsively yanking open the first door she passed. She was inside, with the door pulled shut before she realized she'd taken refuge in some sort of closet.

The door had closed with a metallic clang that reverberated in the small space. Immediately, Laurel tightened her grip on the brass doorknob, twisting it and pushing her shoulder against the solid wood at the same time. The knob hardly budged and the door not at all. All the air left her body at once, turning her muscles tight and immovable. She wrapped her arms stiffly around herself, and the creeping sense of dread that stirred inside her made her panic of a moment ago seem like fun and frolic.

The roots of this fear lay deep in her childhood. This closet, like that other one branded into her memory, was stuffy and windowless. She was surrounded by blackness, and she started to shiver and sweat at the same time, just the way she had on those long-ago "visits" to her Great-Aunt Bessie's house. The invitations had invariably corresponded to spring and fall cleaning times, and Laurel had been more of a housemaid than house guest.

She'd been only ten the first time she'd been sent to Aunt Bessie's, but she learned quickly that the punishment doled out by her spinster aunt for the slightest infraction was a "meditation period" in the locked front hall closet. Try as she might, there was always something she'd failed to do that was deemed of immense importance by her aunt . . . like dusting between the keys on the piano or flipping over the sofa cushions after vacuuming them. Then, terrified but obedient, Laurel would enter the closet, covering her ears to block out the horrifying sound of the old metal key turning on the other side. She'd always heard it anyway and that sound—so like the sound she'd just heard—could trigger terror in her like nothing else ever had.

Laurel was never sure how long her aunt had locked

her in there. She knew it had felt like hours. She'd also learned quickly that crying or calling out only prolonged the ordeal. So she would stand with her back pressed to the door as wave after wave of fear swept over her— fear that her aunt would forget about her, fear that the house would burn down with her still in it, fear that each shuddering breath would be her last.

That's how she felt now—as if there wasn't enough air in the tiny black space to fill her lungs even one more time. The burning tightness in her chest suddenly snapped whatever force was holding her motionless. Raising both fists, she pounded as hard as she could on the solid wood door.

"Help, please, somebody. I'm locked in here . . . in the closet. Please, help. Please . . ." Her cries got weaker as they became mixed with muffled sobs. "Please, you have to get me out of here."

On the other side of the door the sound of her shuddering, breathless sobs were like someone clamping a wrench on Sawyer's heart and twisting.

He pressed up against the door. "I'm here, Laurel. It's Sawyer. I'm going to get you out, baby."

"Sawyer? Oh God, Sawyer, help me, please. Get me out of here."

She began pounding again, the same frantic sound that had caught his attention in the first place. Christ, how had she of all people managed to get stuck in a closet? There was only one possible explanation; she'd seen him waiting up ahead and had been trying to avoid him. Sawyer took no satisfaction in the irony of her situation. He'd wanted to corner Laurel, sure, and make her listen to a few things she was going to hate like the devil hearing, but not like this.

To anyone else, getting locked in there would have been an uncomfortable, mildly embarrassing predicament to be chuckled over later. To Laurel, it was worse than a resurrection of all the goblins in all the nightmares she'd ever had. And he just might be the only person in the world she'd ever told why.

"Laurel, listen to me," he instructed, putting his lips close to the door and keeping his voice easy. "I'm going to get you out, sweetheart, but you have to help me. This is one of those old-fashioned doors with a skeleton key."

He winced, wondering if that was the wrong thing to say, if it would only push her deeper into a world of bad memories. The only sound he heard through the heavy door was her rapid breathing. "Laurel, the key must have fallen when you opened the door," he continued slowly, "and it's not out here, so I want you to look and see if it's on the floor in there somewhere."

"I can't look," she cried. "It's dark in here. Oh, Sawyer, it's so dark. You have to help me."

"I will, baby, trust me." Those words held more of an edge for him than ever. God, if she never trusted him before or after this, let her trust him now. "I know you can't see the key, Laurel, but maybe you can feel for it with your hands...or even your feet. Slide them around the bottom of the door and—"

"I can't, Sawyer," she broke in. Her voice was tight and high-pitched, with none of the sensual huskiness that always managed to stroke his senses with pleasure even when she was berating him for something. "I just can't find it."

Sawyer squeezed his eyes shut and forced himself to think. Of course, she couldn't find it; she was probably too frozen with fear to even move. And he knew from what she'd told him that the longer she was in there the worse it would get. And the longer it would take her to get over it afterward. He'd give everything he owned right down to his soul to spare her even one nightmare.

Uttering reassuring words he hoped would keep her from further panic, he checked the other doors within sight to see if any had the same lock and key. They didn't, and he wasn't sure about the closets in the bedrooms. To check, he would have to leave her alone. The same held true for trying to find one of the household staff for help. The fastest way he could think of to free her was to break the door down. He leaned into it experimentally. Rock solid. But the way the adrenaline was pumping through him, he was sure he could do it.

What held him back was the fact that shattering one of Dane's fancy doors would definitely lead to questions and explanations and certain embarrassment for Laurel. God knows, he'd already put enough pressure on her the last few days, and if she'd just come clean with Dane, as he suspected she had, she wasn't in any state to handle more. The next best way—and the least embarrassing for Laurel—would be to run upstairs and get the pocketknife he had in his suitcase.

"All right, Laurel," he said in a calm, measured tone. "I've thought of a way to get the door open without the key. But to do it, I'm going to have to leave you alone for a—"

"No." The single word was a terror-riddled plea that tightened the wires already twisted around his heart. "Don't leave me, Sawyer."

"I have to, sweetheart. It's the only way I know to get you out. You have to trust me, Laurel, and stay calm and I'll be back before you know it. This time you have to trust me. Can you do that for me, baby?"

Somehow the desperation in his voice penetrated the ocean of fear that threatened to smother Laurel. He was asking her to trust him for her sake, not his own. He was asking her to put her trust in him and not slip over the edge of hysteria, which seemed to be moving closer each second. If ever he had a chance for revenge, she realized numbly, he had it now. He could just walk away, leaving her shivering in the darkness until her screams brought someone else to the rescue. Someone who would have no way of knowing why she was reduced to emotional collapse by such a stupid accident. Only Sawyer knew. And he was doing everything he could to make the ordeal easier for her.

In that instant, love for him welled up inside her, easing her panic long enough for her to draw enough breath to speak.

"I trust you, Sawyer. I do," she whispered, just barely loud enough to be heard through the door. "But hurry, will you?"

"You know me," he countered, and his familiar rough-edged drawl ran like silk over her ragged nerves. "Faster than the speed of sound."

It was an old joke between them. And when the stilted sound of Laurel's brief laugh ended, she knew he was gone. Pressing herself tightly against the door, she closed her eyes and focused her mind on the image of Sawyer's face. It was so easy, as if she had thousands of brain cells dedicated to that task only, saturated with knowledge of the exact depth of the laugh lines that appeared whenever he smiled, and the way his blue eyes narrowed and turned dark with arousal. Gradually, the feeling she'd had earlier, when she'd told Jasper the truth, reclaimed her, and she realized with a start that somehow that sense of peace and her love for Sawyer were intrinsically linked.

The sound of metal jarred her from her daydream only a split second before the door was wrenched open from the other side. Laurel tumbled straight into Sawyer's arms as they closed around her with unquestionable possession.

"You're okay now, baby," he murmured again and again, rubbing his lips against the soft satin of her hair. "You're okay."

She was, and she bubbled with impatience to tell him just how okay. She tilted her head back to smile at him, loving the strong line of his jaw, the sensual pout of his mouth, even the way he breathed, for heaven's sake.

For the first time since he'd reappeared in her life, she set her heart free, making no effort at all to tame the feelings of adoration that came from just looking at him.

"Thank you, Sawyer. God, that was awful," she said with a shudder that disappeared as soon as she rested her head against the solid strength of his chest.

"I know."

"I'm not sure what would have happened to me if you hadn't heard me when you did."

"Shhh." His hand stroked her back, making all the nerves there dance with anticipation. "Don't talk about it."

"I won't." She looked up, meeting his gaze with a resolved expression. "Because there's something much more important I have to talk to you about." Drawing a deep breath, she said, "Sawyer, I was wrong . . . so wrong and unfair to you. And I'm sorry. I don't know how to tell you how sorry I am."

"You just did," he declared softly, his smile tender and loving, without a trace of recrimination. "Subject closed."

"Just like that?" she asked, amazed.

His smile became a full grin, wide and spontaneous. "Just like that."

"Why? How can you possibly forgive me so quickly after all the horrible things I said to you?"

"I said a few horrible things as well," he reminded her.

"Out of self-defense."

"It doesn't matter. I can forgive you anything, always and completely, because I love you."

His hand trapped her jaw, holding her head still. His mouth dipped and applied the most delicate pressure until she parted her lips for him. His tongue filled her mouth, plundering sweetly, practicing the deep, slow thrusts that splintered her soul until she was nothing but ragged pieces of desire, all aimed at him alone.

When he finally lifted his head, she was breathless. Gently, he swept the errant strands of hair from her face. His gaze touched her mouth, her throat, then coasted back to meet her dazzled green eyes. Waiting, it seemed to Laurel.

"I . . . Sawyer, I . . ." The words she should say back to him, which she *wanted* to say because she suddenly knew they were true, sped from her heart to her tongue and then got stuck there, trapped behind a wall of caution and inhibition that was years thick.

"Don't." Sawyer pressed his fingertips against her lips and silenced her stuttering. "Not until you're ready, Laurel. I can wait. Besides, at this moment, there's something I want from you much more than words—I want some action."

Laurel's eyes widened. The sensual invitation in his voice shocked and delighted her. With her emotions already on high, his kiss had incited a longing that suddenly became a physical demand, arcing from her breasts outward with gnawing intensity.

Catching the sparkle of excitement in her eyes, Sawyer laughed. "Yeah, I'll want that, too, eventually. Right now, though, I have a slightly less erotic proposal for you. Run away with me Laurel."

"What?"

"You heard me. I asked you to run away with me . . . right now. We're older and, I hope, a little wiser." His mouth made a smile. "Maybe this time we'll get it right."

"I can't," she burst out.

He didn't react with the slightest surprise or irritation. He simply inquired very matter-of-factly, "Why not?"

"Because . . ." There were hundreds of reasons, Laurel was certain. If only she could zero in on one.

"Laurel," Sawyer sighed, dragging his fingers through his hair in budding exasperation. "I know it's hard for you to just plunge into something without talking and planning and more talking and making lists and schedules and then more talking, but you just can't handle this that way."

"I don't know any other way," she admitted haltingly.

"Let me show you." With his hand cupping her head, he pressed her face into his neck and held her that way, rocking her slightly in his arms. The mingled scent of woods and man tickled her senses. "Sweetheart, we're going to have our share of problems, but we don't need to draw a damn road map to point them out before we even get to them. That would be like living on the edge of disaster all the time."

Laurel drew back to look at him, a tremulous smile breaking through her grim expression. "I've gotten pretty good at that."

"Well, now I'm going to teach you to be good at a lot of other things. Starting right now." His expression sobered, and he loosened his hold marginally. "I gathered that you were in Dane's office all that time making a clean breast of things?"

Laurel nodded.

"And that whatever it was between the two of you is over?"

"Yes. But, Sawyer, there are still other reasons I can't just take off..." Such as gut-level fear, she refrained from saying. He would really howl at that.

"Name one," Sawyer prodded.

"My job."

"Quit," he shot back. "Before they can you. And they will, you know. Reynolds will have no choice but to let you go... at least temporarily."

"I still owe him an explanation," she maintained.

"Fine. Explanation doesn't mean personal appearance. You can call him from wherever we happen to be first thing Monday morning."

"And where will we be?" she asked, finally closing in on the real reason for her reluctance and fear. "Back in Beaumont?"

He was still holding her, massaging her shoulders with a firm, hypnotic touch. "Not by Monday, I shouldn't think. But eventually. That's my home, Laurel," he said softly. "And yours." He lightened his tone. "Besides, I thought talking over old times with Maureen this morning might have made you a little homesick."

Laurel glanced up questioningly. "Old times?"

"Sure. Isn't that what you were doing?"

"No. We were talking about . . . other things," she finished vaguely.

"Well, anyway, Maureen went to Beaumont High, too. Her maiden name was Maureen Riley, and she was a year ahead of me. Of course, her hair wasn't blond back then, but I still thought you recognized her at the reception the other night. You looked so . . . stricken when we walked in."

"That's because I was jealous," she admitted in a sheepish voice. "And because I knew I had to face you with all those ugly accusations—*false* and ugly accusations, as it turns out."

"At least you faced me. You didn't run away this time."

She rested her forehead on his chest for a moment, then lifted it abruptly. "What about Maureen? Did she recognize me?"

"She didn't say, and I didn't ask." At her curious look, Sawyer added, "That would have led to questions about your name, and I gave you my word I wouldn't discuss that with anyone."

"Right," Laurel murmured, awed by the depth of his loyalty, horrified that she could have misjudged him so badly.

"Did it ever occur to you, Laurel," inquired Sawyer,

watching her face intently, "that most folks back in Beaumont don't remember Pandora Milinkus any more than you remembered Maureen?"

It hadn't. But she thought about it now with a dawning insight into the human capacity for inflicting misery inward. Examined through the buffer of time, the things that had seemed so excruciatingly humiliating to her when she'd experienced them were really trivial . . . not nearly the sort of juicy scandalous tidbits that live on in a town's memory for years.

"You mean I was never as big a deal as I thought?" she asked him, her smile one of rueful self-awareness.

"I mean that the power of anything or anyone to hurt you has always been right here"—he touched her forehead—"and here." His fingertips lightly brushed the soft flesh over her heart. "It was never what other people thought that hurt you, Laurel, not really. It was what you thought of yourself. You never thought you were good enough, or pretty enough, or rich enough. I think that, without knowing it, that's what you were trying to tell me the other night. That you had to get away from Beaumont—and maybe from me, too—to have a chance to change, to grow."

"Maybe that was my first mistake," she acknowledged. "Maybe I should have been strong enough to stay and do my growing and changing right there." Her smile had a forlorn, wistful quality. "If I had, things would be so different for us now."

"Different? Yes. Better? We'll never know. This way we've been given a second chance. We can go on from here."

It suddenly occurred to Laurel that their conversation had cut a winding path to a problem she hadn't even thought about until then. There had been too many other, more immediate concerns blocking it from her view.

"You're right, Sawyer. We have to go on from here,

and that's probably the biggest reason why I can't just pick up and go with you. I'm not sure if it's me you love or Dory. Yes, I went in there and told Jasper the truth, and yes, I plan to straighten out the rest of the mess I made of my life. But that doesn't change who I am now . . . who I *want* to be. I'll still be this person I've grown into, not the girl I was eleven years ago."

He pulled her tightly against him, melding their bodies from shoulder to thigh. "And I love the person you've grown into," he insisted in a husky whisper.

"Maybe," she countered, wishing there was some magic lens she could peer through to be certain of that. "And maybe you'll wake up one morning and realize all you were doing is trying to recapture an old dream."

"That's the thing about love, sweetheart. It doesn't come with any guarantees. Not eleven years ago when I asked you to wait, and not now when I'm asking you to take my hand and walk out of here with me, right this minute, no looking back."

Her teeth scraped across her bottom lip. "Sawyer, I can't."

"Is that your final answer?"

"Yes . . . I don't kn—, yes," she forced herself to say again.

Dropping his arms to his sides, Sawyer shrugged. "All right. If that's the way you want it."

Laurel's heart hit her heels. He was leaving, no pleading, no arguments. She was losing him all over again.

Before she could say anything, and without a word of warning, Sawyer bent down, slipped one arm behind her knees and swung her up into his arms. Heading for the front door, his stride was brisk, his tone laconic. "Just never let me hear it said that I didn't ask first."

Chapter Ten

"WAIT. HOLD IT. Stop! What do you think you're doing?" Laurel swiveled her head to see around Sawyer's imposing shoulders, cringing to think there might be a witness to this embarrassingly prehistoric display.

"What I should have done years ago," he replied calmly, working the front door open with one hand and bounding down the wide brick steps. "Ignoring what you say you want and giving you a shot at what you really do want but are too scared to go after."

"Oooh." She reared back and glared at his infuriatingly serene expression. You would think her heart-pounding agitation would be at least slightly contagious. "What a typically arrogant, swaggering male thing to say. As if you know what a woman wants better than she does herself."

"Uh-uh. I don't know squat about women," he professed, shaking his head with an air which contrived to seem downright humble. Laurel was not fooled. "Except for you, that is."

Her smile was tart. "And I suppose you think that what I want is you?"

"Bingo. To be precise, I think you want me *almost* as much as I want you."

In spite of her irritation, the remark filled Laurel with a pleasant, suffusing heat. Turning her head to hide any evidence of it from him, she retorted, "Lucky me."

"I'm glad you feel that way." His voice was a sexy growl. "Because for a while, it's going to be just the two of us."

She jerked her gaze back to him, still more annoyed than alarmed. The careless, almost playful slant to his manner led her to believe he wouldn't actually go through with this crazy abduction. And she had to admit, there was something unabashedly romantic about being swept away in the arms of the man you loved. Provided, of course, that in the end the man heeded your command to halt. They were circling the house, heading in the direction of the garages at the end of the drive, and she figured it was nearing time for a final, no-nonsense protest.

"Sawyer, you realize, of course, that you can't do this," she ventured.

He grinned.

"Sawyer. This isn't funny."

"No kidding. It isn't much fun either. You're not as light as you look, kid."

"Then put me down, damn it."

She tried to twist free, only to have him tighten his hold, pressing her closer to his chest. Out of the corner of her eye, she noticed one of the caretakers standing by the corner of the garage. He was young and wearing a go-for-it grin as he watched Sawyer stride across the yard with her in his arms.

"Sawyer, please don't make a scene," she ordered through clenched teeth.

"I don't have to. You're making enough of one for both of us."

Laurel quickly forced herself to stop struggling. It was a bit harder to summon forth the tight smile intended to convince any observers that this was some sort of silly little game. Personally, she was beginning to have her doubts about that.

"This is ridiculous, Sawyer. You can't just carry me off against my will this way."

He quickly shifted his arms, tossing her over his shoulder fireman-style. "Do you like being carried off this way any better?"

"No."

"Tough. From my end it's great."

The sundress she was wearing was made of soft, washed cotton, a flimsy barrier against the quick erotic attack his teeth made on the tender flesh of her backside. The wiggle of her hips that resulted was entirely beyond Laurel's control.

"Ow!" Her head shot up as, mortified, she scanned the grounds to see if anyone had witnessed *that*. Luckily, they'd made enough progress to be shielded from view by the side of the garage.

"You . . . you bit me," she exclaimed.

"Yeah, and you liked it. I'll have to remember that."

He came to a sudden halt and unceremoniously dumped her from his shoulder to the front seat of a car that Laurel presumed was his. It was a convertible, with the top down, and Sawyer didn't waste time using the door to reach the driver's seat. The sight of his lean, agile body sliding in next to her was startlingly familiar to Laurel. She'd seen him make that same smooth leap hundreds of times before, and for a few seconds a reluctant smile pierced her frown.

The powerful roar of the car's engine as Sawyer

twisted the key shattered the nostalgic moment, and along with it any remaining illusions that he was only playing. Shifting into reverse, he swung the car around, then shot forward. Briefly Laurel considered jumping to freedom, but dismissed the idea as he rapidly accelerated, taking the twisting drive with a negligent skill that was also familiar.

Numb with disbelief, she watched the stately white columns in front of the Dane estate shrink to toothpicks in the distance. Finally turning away from the streak of green and gold the landscape had become, she stared at his rough-hewn profile. "You're doing it. I didn't think . . . I can't believe you're actually doing it. This," she declared, "is kidnapping."

"You are one very observant lady," Sawyer drawled. Then he shot her an expectant smile. "Just like old times, huh?"

"No," she snapped. "Those were dates, Sawyer. This is . . . at least a felony."

"Adds excitement, don't you think?"

"No."

He shrugged, looking a little disappointed by her lack of enthusiasm for being shanghaied. "That's too bad. I guess I'll just have to try harder to excite you."

"Don't do me any favors."

"Think nothing of it. It will be my pleasure."

Turning from him with a disgusted sound, she sat with her back pressed to the seat, her arms folded stiffly across her chest, staring straight ahead. The numbness of disbelief was beginning to fade and she was rapidly heating to a simmering stage of anger.

"They'll be worried, you know," she pointed out, grappling for something that might change his mind. "We left in such a *hurry;* I didn't tell anyone I was leaving."

"You can call and leave a message when we make our first pit stop."

"And I don't have anything with me . . . not even a toothbrush."

"We'll buy whatever you need along the way. I did consider giving you a chance to pack," he explained, "but then I would have lost the element of surprise."

"Some surprise," Laurel muttered. There was a long silence. "Have you given any thought to where we're running away *to?*"

Shrugging, Sawyer answered, "No. But I'm open to suggestions."

"Good, I have one. Turn around."

"Try again."

Laurel flashed him a syrupy smile. "No, I don't think you'd like my other suggestion about where you can go any better."

His laugh was a deep, rough sound that rubbed all her nerves the wrong way. Glancing sideways at her, he reached over and caressed the curve of her chin, laughing again softly, when she pulled away.

"Come on, Laurel," he cajoled. "What's done is done. Why don't you cheer up?"

"Why don't you shut up?" she snapped in return.

"Okay, I will."

He calmly reached for the radio dial, fiddling with it until he found a station that played country music, then settling back to drive with one hand on the wheel, his elbow propped on the door beside him. The cheerful, almost chivalrous way he took her bitchy remark in stride robbed every ounce of satisfaction from it and left Laurel feeling, of all things, guilty. Which was ludicrous. After all, she thought irritably, she was the victim here. Which made Sawyer the villain.

Only it was hard to take that thought very seriously while he accompanied Merle Haggard with that soft, slightly raspy whistle she'd always found sexy in an out-of-kilter, endearing sort of way. Hearing it had the same effect on her senses as stroking the back of his neck or cradling his head in her lap used to. It made her feel linked to him in a special, timeless way she definitely did not want to feel at this moment.

Resolutely, she kept her eyes directed away from the subversive sight of his angular hand on the wheel or the relaxed V-shape of his thighs. Instead, she stared blankly at the monotonous scenery, doing her best to block out both Sawyer's whistle and Haggard's worn voice singing: "Let's chase each other 'round the room tonight. Let's play the kind of games we played on our wedding night."

It was a challenge, but by continually reminding herself of the sheer indignity of being tossed over his shoulder and hauled away like some prize calf, she managed to steam her way through Virginia and a good part of Maryland. Somewhere just inside Pennsylvania, though, she reached the grim conclusion that it's a chore to keep anger burning brightly without a steady supply of fuel. And Sawyer's cheerful silence didn't provide much in the way of that. As the ride dragged on relentlessly, her feelings of animosity waned and her physical discomfort increased.

The farmland of rural Pennsylvania gave way to the rolling foothills of the Adirondacks as they crossed into western New York State. Still, Sawyer didn't suggest stopping, and Laurel stubbornly refused to be the first to break the silence by asking . . . even if her need for a ladies' room was growing more urgent with each rest stop they whizzed past. Finally, sometime after five, he pulled off the freeway and into the parking lot of a small shopping center, which included a gas station and sandwich shop. There was also a phone booth out front.

Sawyer parked, climbed out of the car, and stretched. "You can call Dane if you want to," he said to her as pleasantly as if they hadn't just driven over two hundred miles in silence.

Laurel ignored him.

"Let me put that another way. Either you call or I will. He deserves to know you're all right."

"I'm not all right," she couldn't resist shouting back.

"Fine. Then tell him that. Tell him I kidnapped you and drove you across state lines . . . several of them, actually." Reaching into his jeans pocket, he flipped her a quarter. "Be sure to take a look when you get out so you can give him the license plate number and a description of the getaway vehicle, too."

It was not the angry outburst Laurel would have found so satisfying. Watching him amble off in the direction of the men's room, she glumly realized that was because he wasn't angry. He wasn't even particularly annoyed by her bad mood. He was just 100 percent sure that she wouldn't tell Jasper anything of the sort. And, of course, he was right. First, because it would just be too embarrassing. And secondly, because it wasn't exactly the truth.

Honesty made her admit that if she had really kicked up a fuss, Sawyer—the man who had exhibited such tender concern for her when she'd been locked in the closet—would have turned back. It also made her own up to the fact that her protest had been a bit on the . . . obligatory side. And much as it galled Laurel to even think it, maybe it was because Sawyer was right. Was it possible that deep down she really did want to go with him, but was afraid to let it happen?

Slamming the car door on that disturbing possibility, she sought out the ladies' room before calling Jasper. When she finally called, his housekeeper answered, and Laurel decided the simplest way to handle it was to ask her to relay to Jasper her apology for leaving so suddenly, as well as a request that her luggage be sent to her apartment.

Preoccupied with her own tangled thoughts, she was halfway back to the car before she looked at it. Really looked at it, that is, for the first time. She'd been too busy damning Sawyer's existence earlier to much care what he was driving, and besides, she couldn't see a whole lot of it from the inside. Now she stopped in the middle of the parking lot and let her gaze slide from fender to gleaming fender, taking in every familiar inch of shiny red paint and glistening chrome in between.

It was a Chevy. A red 1962 Chevy convertible, to be exact. She'd recognize it anywhere. It sat there in the setting sun like a shrine to some of the happiest days of her life.

Nearly running the rest of the way, she stopped beside the passenger door and looked at Sawyer, who was already lounging behind the wheel, waiting for her.

"I noticed you called Dane," he remarked. "Good girl."

Laurel hardly heard what he said. "Sawyer, this car —it's a '62 Chevy."

Her voice was vibrant with excitement, and the corners of Sawyer's mouth lifted in response.

"You noticed," he drawled. "Hallelujah! I was beginning to think I'd spoken too soon when I said you were observant."

"A *red* '62 Chevy. Is it . . ."

"The same car?" he interjected. "No. But it just may be the only survivor of the species in the whole country. Until the day before yesterday, it was painted white and living a quiet life of retirement somewhere in North Carolina."

Laurel's laughter rippled in the cool, early evening air. "So this is what Maureen meant when she said you were going crazy looking for a car."

"Maureen didn't know exactly what kind of car, though. I figured no one but you would ever understand why I had to have this particular model." His eyes drifted over her face as unhurried and as stimulating as a caress. When he spoke, it was in a voice that was husky and pitched low. "You can't go chasing after an old dream in just anything, you know. If you want to catch it, everything has to be exactly right."

Laurel stared at him with a wide-eyed look of wonderment. "You had this whole thing planned."

"More or less."

"I thought it was a mad impulse," she confessed. "Something you might come to regret . . . an act of passion."

"Let's call it a well-planned act of passion," Sawyer countered, his smile alluring. Reaching over, he shoved her door open. "Are you getting in?"

She did, this time of her own volition, and Sawyer steered the car onto the two-lane road that led back to the highway.

"Hungry?" he asked after they'd driven about half a mile. Lifting from the seat between them a brown paper bag that had gone unnoticed by Laurel, he held it out to her.

She grinned at him. "Don't tell me there are donuts in this bag?"

"Sorry," he said with a regretful wince. "This nostaglia stuff is all well and good, but I happen to be really hungry. I hope you still like mayonnaise on your roast beef sandwich."

"That sounds . . . delicious."

In her current mood, sandpaper on toast would probably sound delicious. The rolling landscape on both sides was shrouded with evening shadows, but to Laurel the road ahead was looking clearer and brighter. She pulled the sandwiches—and the milkshakes he'd bought to go with them—from the bag, and they ate while he drove along the scenic route that more or less paralleled the highway.

"We can get back on the interstate further up ahead," he explained between hungry bites. "It's easier to eat and drive at thirty miles an hour than it is at fifty."

"I don't mind," Laurel assured him. "Actually, this is

a nice change of pace. If I saw one more *This is the Start of a Measured Mile* sign, I might have screamed."

"I was kind of afraid you were mad enough to scream if I so much as suggested stopping to get a decent meal in a nice restaurant. Otherwise, I never would have fed you a sandwich and a shake for dinner."

"I'm glad you did. I'd rather eat a sandwich alone with you than prime rib in the fanciest restaurant around."

Sawyer didn't say a word in response to her halted admission, but he looked over at her and smiled in a way that said he understood and agreed. They finished eating in silence. Instead of an angry void, however, this time it was the sort of quiet that hummed with satisfaction. And with anticipation. By the time Laurel gathered up the wrappers and empty cups and stowed them back in the bag, the urge to move on to the next step, to bridge this electric gap between them with whatever words had yet to be said, was irrepressible.

"Are we ever going to stop driving?" she finally inquired delicately.

"I've been asking myself that very same question for . . . oh, the last sixty or so miles," Sawyer replied.

"And?"

"And it all depends on you."

Noticing the muscles of his throat move as he took a hard swallow, Laurel experienced a cool rush of trepidation. Then he reached over and took her hand, enclosing it in his warm, textured grasp, and she felt strength and confidence and love explode inside. It was as if they'd been in her all along, like tiny compressed sponges, waiting for the ocean of miracles that was Sawyer to make them bloom.

"Laurel, ever since I crashed back into your life, I've been pressuring you, crowding you. Making you spend time alone with me, making love to you . . ."

"Sawyer, you hardly forced . . ."

"You weren't ready." His words rang with finality. "Not really. If you had been, you wouldn't have panicked the way you did the next morning." He shook his head. "I just wanted you so damn much."

"I can understand that," Laurel said softly.

The tight lines around his eyes relaxed into a quick smile. "Thank you. But the fact remains that I've been bullying you, Laurel. I've wanted everything my own way. I even manipulated events this week to force a showdown between you and Dane. Because I was jealous," he confessed with a sheepish shrug.

Laurel's expression held a fine edge of sadness. "Is that why you went to Riordon with information about Jasper's past?"

His head shook firmly. "That's just it. I went to Mike to *stop* him from going public with it. It's true that I came to Washington determined to block Dane's confirmation—in fact, the whole time I was here I had Maureen and others on my staff searching for information to do just that."

"And they dug back far enough to find out about his father," Laurel supplied in a monotone.

Sawyer nodded. "When Maureen couldn't reach me at the hotel to tell me she'd come up with something, she called Mike's office and left the message with him. Mike thought just the hint of a scandal would get Dane to withdraw. But by then, I'd found you again, and the only thing I cared about was getting you back in my life. I'd scrap that North Sea deal ten times over," he said emphatically, "if that's what it took to have a chance with you."

Laurel gazed at him in bewilderment, trying to mesh what he was saying with the pieces of the puzzle she already had. If what he seemed to be telling her was true, there might be enough happy ending here to go around.

"Are you telling me that you and Mike aren't going to reveal what you know about Jasper?"

"That's right, we're not. From the start, Mike was only bowing to pressure from powerful local constituents . . . namely me," he acknowledged. "Once I made it clear I'd changed my mind on the matter, he was agreeable to calling a halt to our plan. Win or lose, I won't have a thing to do with Dane's confirmation."

"Then whoever spoke to Bill must have misinterpreted what he overheard you discussing with Mike," Laurel murmured, thinking out loud.

"What was that?"

"It doesn't matter. Did you really decide all this because of me?" she asked, almost afraid to believe his love for her was powerful enough to make him abandon a project that could have earned him a fortune.

Sawyer took his eyes off the road to look at her, the answer to her fears radiating from his unshuttered expression. He nodded. "I was afraid that if I went ahead with the plan to destroy Dane's chances, you would think exactly what you did—that my motives were tied in with my feelings for you, with that crazy notion of yours that I was out for revenge. I know you well enough to know that would only provoke a surge of protectiveness on your part and end up cementing your relationship with Dane."

His gaze suddenly sharpened with determination. "As you've seen, I had my own plans for the outcome of that little farce . . . especially after I found out you were an engaged-to-be-engaged virgin, for pete's sake." His gaze danced quickly, scorchingly over her body. "The man is obviously a fool. And even if you told me to go to hell once and for all, there was no way I was going to do anything that might back you into going through with a marriage that was all wrong for you out of guilt or misplaced loyalty or something."

If she hadn't known it before, Laurel knew at that

moment that she loved him, really loved him, then and forever. The truth of it shot through her like a laser.

"You're right, you certainly do like getting your own way." Her tone caressed him, her eyes adored him, but Sawyer was too wound up to notice.

"But not this time," he said with conviction. "That's what I meant when I said it's up to you when we stop and how and where. I may have picked the game by dragging you off this way, but you're making the rules from here on out. I told you that I love you, Laurel. That's the truth. I'll be just as up front about what I want. I want *you,* tonight and every night for the rest of my life . . . even longer if I can figure out a way. I want you naked, under me, over me, as wild and as giving as you were that first night."

His words took Laurel's breath away, but it didn't matter. He didn't give her a chance to speak. His hand held on to hers tightly, as if he was afraid she might cover her ears or run away before he got it all out.

"That may be crude and graphic," he continued hurriedly, "but I want you to know how I feel . . . all of it. I also want to take care of you when you're sick, hold you when you're sad. I want to help with your problems and share mine with you when they come. I want you to have my babies."

His deep voice wavered, hinting at the strain on his tightly leashed emotions. Laurel hadn't been aware of the rigidity of the muscles of his shoulders and arms until they relaxed suddenly. The tension seemed to fall away from him like autumn leaves off an oak.

"Let's see, you want wild sex, sickness and health, and babies. Is that all?" she asked, dry humor in her voice.

Sawyer shot her an incredulous look that gradually made room for a tentative smile. "Those are the high points."

"Okay. I think I can handle all that," she said with a thoughtful nod.

"What the hell does that mean?" he growled.

"It means you can stop anytime now. I'm not angry anymore."

"Damn it, woman, was that a yes?"

She arched her brows. "Did you ask a question?"

"Yeah, eleven years ago, and I'm still waiting for you to get the answer right."

"Do you think you could repeat the question?"

"No," he drawled with a slow smile, letting their speed dwindle almost to a halt. Laurel was more glad than ever they'd stuck to the lightly traveled scenic route. The way Sawyer was dividing his attention between the road and her . . . with Laurel gradually receiving the bulk of it, any encounter with another car could be fatal. "I think that for the sake of accuracy, you better do the repeating," he ordered. "Say yes, I'll marry you, Sawyer."

"Yes, I'll marry you, Sawyer."

A wide grin slashed across his mouth. "I love you, Sawyer."

Laurel ran her tongue over her lips and echoed softly, "I love you, Sawyer. I love you, I love you."

"I want you, Sawyer," he said, his husky tone barely audible over the thundering of her heart.

"I want you, Sawyer. Naked. Under me, over me, wild and giving."

She slid across the seat, twining one arm around his neck and toying with the buttons on his shirt with her other hand just as Sawyer slammed on the brakes. He kept her from flying over the windshield by wrapping both arms around her tightly enough to crush ribs, and it was a few seconds before Laurel realized that wasn't his primary reason for stopping.

While she wasn't looking, the road they were on seemed to have narrowed considerably until it simply dead-ended in a moss-covered mound about fifteen feet in front of them. Beyond that stretched what looked like an overgrown pasture. On both sides of them the land was slightly more hilly and wooded. All of it was dark and deserted.

"I think I took the wrong fork in the road somewhere," Sawyer observed after a moment.

"Were there any signs?"

"I don't know. I was watching you." He shut off the engine. "You did say you wanted to stop."

"This isn't exactly what I had in mind."

"What did you have in mind?" he asked, settling her so close to his side that there wasn't a fraction of an inch of red vinyl seat left between them. Her shoulder fit snugly under his, and her head found its own way to that spot on his chest that felt as if it had been created just to cradle it. "A truck stop on the interstate? No? Maybe something with more ambience. We passed a place called the Rose Glow Motel about ten miles back. The sign said they have waterbeds and triple-X movies."

"Actually," she said, turning her body to his, "I think I'm beginning to like the ambience here just fine."

It was true. His hand was dusting over her arm in a caress that made all her senses whir to life. She felt the past tugging at her pleasantly. She and Sawyer, alone in a parked car on a warm spring night. It brought back memories, all right.

"I only wonder what a cop would say if he came along and found us parking out here?" she mused. "Especially in this relic from our youth."

"He'd probably say that for a typical swaggering, arrogant male kidnapper I have great taste in women."

His hand that had been rubbing her arm slid across her breast to slip open the top button on her bodice.

"Did I really call you that?" Laurel murmured, her

heart giving a small leap of excitement as his deft
fingers freed the second small button as well.

"Or else something very close to it."

"I was upset."

"I could tell." Warm fingers penetrated the opening
they had created and closed around the full globe of her
breast. A sharp intake of breath signaled his surprise
and pleasure at discovering she wasn't wearing a bra
beneath the narrow-strapped sundress. "And what are
you now?"

"Dizzy," she breathed, smiling. "And very glad that
you're an arrogant male who also happens to be strong
enough to carry me off against my will."

"Barely," he reminded her, his tone teasing and loving.

"Swine," retorted Laurel, tilting her head up to him
with a laugh that faded instantly at the intense hunger
she read on his face.

"Say that again." His words were a gruff command,
but his eyes, burning brightly in the darkness, held a
smoky, unmistakable invitation. It was echoed and am-
plified by his fingers, plucking sweetly, maddeningly, at
the puckered tip of her breast.

She parted her lips to obey. But before a sound
escaped, Sawyer's mouth covered hers, swallowing the
word and replacing it with the bold, thrusting warmth of
his tongue. His timing was perfect. Laurel was soft and
relaxed from her laughter. She closed her eyes and surrendered to the moment, to the night, to Sawyer and the
insistent, reckless passion of his kiss.

His mouth was masterful. Again and again he kissed
her, with strokes that were long and deep, and with delicate flicks of his tongue that had her yearning for more.
Mindlessly, Laurel heeded the silent direction of his
hands as he turned her to face him. When her bared
breasts teased the muscled terrain of his chest, Sawyer
groaned from deep within him. With increasing ur-

gency, his hands swept down her sides, spanning the narrowness of her ribs, then back up to frame the full sides of her breasts while his thumbs massaged their velvety crests.

When his lips moved away from hers, his hands lingered on her body, touching, exploring, sustaining the desire that was making her insides quiver with impatience.

"I love you, Laurel," he whispered. "And I want to make love to you."

"The Rose Glow Motel is only ten miles away," she reminded him, moving sinuously against him.

"The only problem," he countered, his voice hoarse as he pressed closer, rubbing her belly with the hard shaft behind the zipper of his jeans, "is that I don't have ten miles of self-control left in me."

Laurel's eyes widened with excitement as she felt the glorious proof of just how urgent his need for her was. The feminine counterpart of his passion trembled inside her, from the tips of her pleasured breasts to the soft, liquid ache between her thighs.

"Is this the same man who wanted plenty of time and plenty of room?" she asked playfully as her fingers began unbuttoning his shirt in a very direct declaration of her intentions.

"Time, we have," murmured Sawyer, arching with pleasure as her palms swirled across his chest, then over his smooth shoulders, dragging his shirt with them. "All the time in the world. As for room, that was only a hard and fast requirement for the first time. Now I'm ready for variety."

Laurel dipped her head and ran her tongue over his nipples, smiling at their quick response. "Hard and fast, hmmm?" The light flick of her tongue moved down his chest and flirted with the forest of hair above his belt. Her chin brushed the tip of the perpendicular ridge just below. "I think I'd rather have it hard and slow."

Sawyer's hands gripped her shoulders to pull her up to him. His smile was sexy, his eyes adoring as he growled, "One night and you've turned into a wanton."

"Mmm-hmm. Aren't you glad?"

"Ecstatic," he murmured, tilting his head to nuzzle her neck. "Just remember, two can play this game."

Never taking his eyes from hers, he brought her hand to his mouth and rubbed his lips back and forth across her knuckles, leaving them moist and tingling. Before he did it, Laurel couldn't have imagined such an innocuous caress causing this steadily tightening spiral of desire down low in her belly. Now she couldn't imagine any other caress ever being so sweetly arousing.

Then slowly he rotated her hand and swirled his tongue in her slightly cupped palm and she knew she was wrong. This was even better. Shudders of pleasure coursed through her as, one by one, he drew her fingertips into his mouth and sucked with a primitive cadence that drove her mad. His tongue picked up the same rhythm and played it up and down the sensitive tips while his dark eyes made endless love to hers.

"Sawyer," she sighed deeply, unconsciously lifting her breasts to him.

Smiling, he lowered his mouth and caught the tip of one between his teeth, nibbling gently, then drawing it deeper and suckling until Laurel was whimpering and clasping his shoulders for support. Goose bumps danced up and down her spine as he moved to her other breast, showering it with the same erotic attention.

With his lips still hot and busy at her breast, his hands eased the straps of her dress off her shoulders, leaving her, like him, naked from the waist up. Lifting his head finally, he gazed at the ivory mounds and red nipples his mouth had made wet. His hand reached out and touched them lightly, reverently, as if to break contact completely would be as painful for him as Laurel knew it would be for her. The sight of his fingers, so strong and dark against her paler flesh, sent her senses rocketing into overdrive.

She reached for him at the same instant he groaned and carried her with him to the opposite end of the seat, away from the obstacle of the steering wheel. His dark gaze roved over her hungrily as, with movements that were unbelievably quick and graceful considering the cramped surroundings, he removed the rest of his clothes. In the small, shadowy confines of the car, the sight of his aroused manhood—full, hard, and as proud as the man himself—affected Laurel even more than ever before.

Her hand closed around him, sliding over the sleek, satiny flesh for only seconds until, with a harsh sound, he twisted away, settling himself on the seat and pulling her down on top of him.

His hand moved over the soft folds of fabric covering her hip. "What are you wearing under this?"

"Not much," Laurel whispered, shivering as he bunched the material and slid his hand underneath to find the skimpy bikini panties she was referring to.

"Good," he countered, his voice low and gravelly as he pulled them down over her thighs, her knees and bare feet. Dropping them to the floor, his fingers climbed her legs again, parting them and finding the in-between place that was sleek and ready for him. He touched her deeply, making himself part of her and causing her to bite down hard on her lip and bury her face in the damp curve of his neck as preliminary spasms began to ripple within her.

"Oh God, baby," he whispered, covering her mouth with his in a ravenous kiss that left them both shaking. Lifting her, he shifted beneath until her legs were poised on either side of his hips. Laurel helped by bracing herself on her knees, then slowly, slowly lowering herself onto him.

Their eyes locked at the moment the tip of his erection touched the velvet portal of her womanhood.

"Now, Laurel," he pleaded. "Please, now."

She sank down on him, welcoming him, letting him fill her completely, and for long moments neither of them moved as they savored the splendor of being one, of reaching the pinnacle of intimacy. Sawyer stirred first, lifting his hips in a way that roused Laurel and made her purr.

They were both too aroused to hold back, to exert the sort of fine control that would prolong their pleasure. Their movements quickened in unison, and with them, their shared need for fulfillment. When Laurel became too overcome to move, Sawyer bracketed her hips with his hands and took full control, driving them both closer to ecstacy. She gave herself up to his hard, sure thrusts with a total outpouring of love. And when the tumult came, she felt him do the same, pouring his life force into her with a surrender that equaled her own.

When the shudders had stopped, Laurel collapsed against him, her muscles as limp as the stuffing in a rag doll. Fine tuning her senses, she tried to hold onto the magic as long as possible. It was a rude, almost painful jolt when the first raindrops splashed on her bare arms.

"What the—?" Sawyer straightened against the seat, evidently feeling it at the same instant she did, and they both looked up just in time to see the scattered, giant drops become a steady stream that seemed to be coming at them from all directions.

"The top," he shouted, lifting her aside and lunging for the button that activated it. He jabbed it twice, and the only response was a painful creaking noise from the vicinity of where the top lay folded up behind the back seat.

"It must be jammed," he muttered, hard on the heels of a more raunchy description of the uncooperative roof. Grabbing his jeans, he yanked them on while Laurel did her best to reassemble her own clothing. Unzipped and unsnapped, he barreled into the back seat, grabbed the resisting top with both hands and tugged.

"Hit the button now," he directed Laurel.

Leaving half her buttons undone, she hurried to obey.

A minute later, after more unsuccessful tugging, he shouted, "Try it again."

Nothing.

"What the hell did they do?" he demanded of the angry sky. "Drip paint on the gears? Check out everything under the hood, I said. Everything. Don't leave a rusty valve or a loose cable in her. So instead they screw up the damn top."

The rain was coming down in torrents, flooding the inside of the car. Laurel, already soaked to the skin, tried in vain to man the switch, shield herself from the hard-hitting drops, and peel away the wet clumps of hair plastered to her face at the same time. Finally giving up on all of it, she slid back to her own seat and looked around at Sawyer.

He was standing in the back, wearing only his unfastened jeans and an outraged expression, and a laugh started building inside Laurel. The whole situation was ridiculous, and no worse than they deserved for behaving like two adolescents with no self-control. She laughed out loud.

"Mind telling me what's so damn funny?" Sawyer demanded, spinning around. His rage was given an added emphasis and full illumination by the lightning that suddenly split the sky.

"I was just thinking about that old saying, 'They don't make them like they used to,'" she explained, mauling the words with gasps of laughter.

For a second, he glared at her in utter disbelief, and that only made her laugh harder. Then his face broke into a grin that was bordered by twin rivulets of rain, and he finally let loose with a roar of laughter that rivaled the thunder in the distance.

"Wrong, Laurel," he said when he could speak again. "It looks like they didn't always make them like they used to even back then."

That said, he stepped over the front seat, sat down with a slosh, and took her mouth in a kiss that was wet and unhurried and a wonderful harbinger of the way they would meet all that came to them in the years ahead, the bitter and the sweet. With Sawyer by her side, Laurel knew she could face anything and conquer it. Even Beaumont.

He finally lifted his head, a wicked look in his eyes that was half question, half promise.

"The Rose Glow Motel?" he asked softly.

Laurel nodded, her slow smile free of all uncertainty. "And step on it."

SECOND CHANCE AT LOVE

COMING NEXT MONTH

CONSPIRACY OF HEARTS #406 by Pat Dalton
Eric Trevor claims he's a spy protecting her
from danger, but Lisa Rollins is captivated by her
mysterious guardian—and that's where the danger lies...

HEAT WAVE #407 by Lee Williams
To Hollywood movie scout Nadine McGuane,
sleeping in the eye of a South American hurricane
seems simple—compared to tangling with
dashing anthropologist Zachary Matthews.

TEMPORARY ANGEL #408 by Courtney Ryan
Stung by hometown gossip and disapproval, Ashley Evans
turns to her platonic male roommate,
sexy musician Jesse Stark, for comfort...but
discovers unspoken passion instead...

HERO AT LARGE #409 by Steffie Hall
When unemployed carpenter Ken Callahan moves in
to perform "house husband" chores for skating coach
Chris Nelson, her heart's in more trouble than his career!

CHASING RAINBOWS #410 by Carole Buck
Paralegal Laura Newton's drawn to debonair, crusading
lawyer Kenyon C. Sutton—but his noble causes soon
bring him to battle with her prestigious Boston firm...

PRIMITIVE GLORY #411 by Cass McAndrew
Amanda Lacey finds that getting field agronomist
Eric Nichols to follow office procedures in the exotic
Himalayas is as impossible as resisting his heated embraces.

Highly Acclaimed
Historical Romances From Berkley

_____ 0-425-09079-5   **A Triumph of Roses**
$3.95   by Mary Pershall
"Five stars." —Affaire de Coeur. From the author of A Shield of Roses
comes a new novel about two lovers caught in a struggle where
surrender means love.

_____ 0-425-09472-3   **Let No Man Divide**
$4.50   by Elizabeth Kary
An alluring belle and a handsome, wealthy ship-builder are drawn
together amidst the turbulence of the Civil War's western front.

_____ 0-425-09218-6   **The Chains of Fate**
$3.95   by Pamela Belle
Warrior and wife torn apart by civil war in England, bravely battle
the chains of fate that separate them.

_____ 0-425- 09333-6   **Blaze**
$3.95   by Susan Johnson
The beautiful, pampered daughter of a Boston millionaire is
taken hostage by a proud Absarokee chief in this sweeping epic
of the Montana frontier.